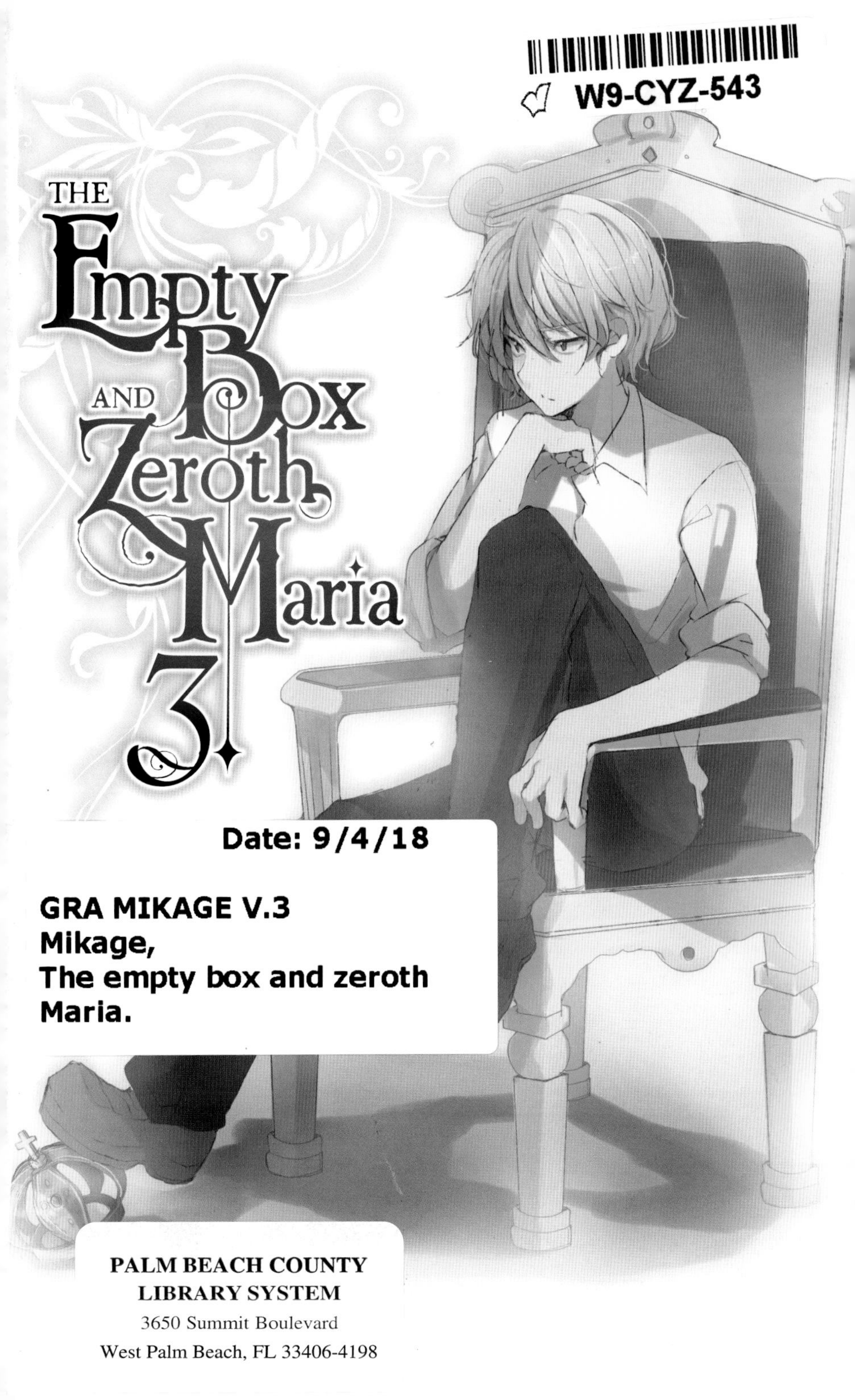
THE
Empty
AND Box
Zeroth
Maria
3

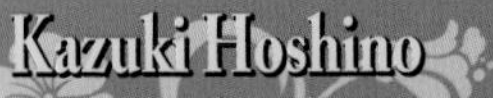

An extremely ordinary young man with a decidedly unusual obsession with maintaining a normal life. He has become a favorite object of study for O. Though he is one of the weakest players in the game, he also has the potential to become a trickster.

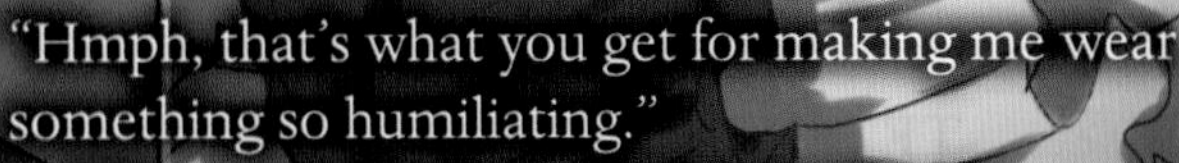

"Hmph, that's what you get for making me wear something so humiliating."

H-hey…you're the one who put it on!

"Still, Kazuki… You look even more… unfortunate than I expected."

"What're you talking about?! *You* forced me to dress like this!"

"You look awful, but it is what it is… Maybe I'll set that picture I just took as my wallpaper."

"Why?!"

"Because it gets you riled up, that's why. Don't make me state the obvious."

That's just sadistic!

Maria Otonashi
A beautiful and heroic young woman on the hunt for O, the granter of Boxes. Though she is gifted in the martial arts and possesses a keen mind, her excessively noble nature has led her to forbid herself from harming others. She is at once the strongest and the weakest player in the game.

"Why're you studying during break, Yuri?!"

"Eep! I-Iroha. H-hello."

"It's a little late for a 'hello' now, don't you think? You haven't answered my question, either."

"Um...I'm not smart like you, so I have to work extra hard."

"That's rich, coming from the one with the best grades... If any of your classmates hear that, they're gonna hate your guts, you know."

"R-really? I-I'm sorry..."

"I'm kidding—no need to apologize! Gosh, so serious. You are too cute."

"...Ngh, you're just making fun of me now."

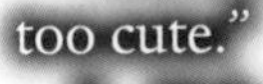

Yuri Yanagi
A shy, quiet, and rather skittish girl with a brilliant mind on par with Iroha's. Her charm and behavior spark the protective instincts of those around her, leading to some unexpected consequences in the game.

Iroha Shindo
The young president of the student council. She has excellent grades and is the ace of the track-and-field club. In the game, she boasts incomparable physical and mental stats.

"……"
"That must be the Daiya I've heard so many stories about. He's handsomer than I expected. But he still can't hold a candle to me!"
Koudai Kamiuchi
A young man who conceals many talents beneath the facade of a lighthearted class clown. He navigates the game by making clever use of his easygoing exterior and well-hidden interior to deceive others.

"……"
"That's gotta be Koudai Kamiuchi from middle school. Yeah, there's something about him I still can't stand."
Daiya Oomine
A cunning cynic with silver hair and earrings. His most dangerous weapon is his ability to deceive and even kill without any qualms if it serves his purpose.

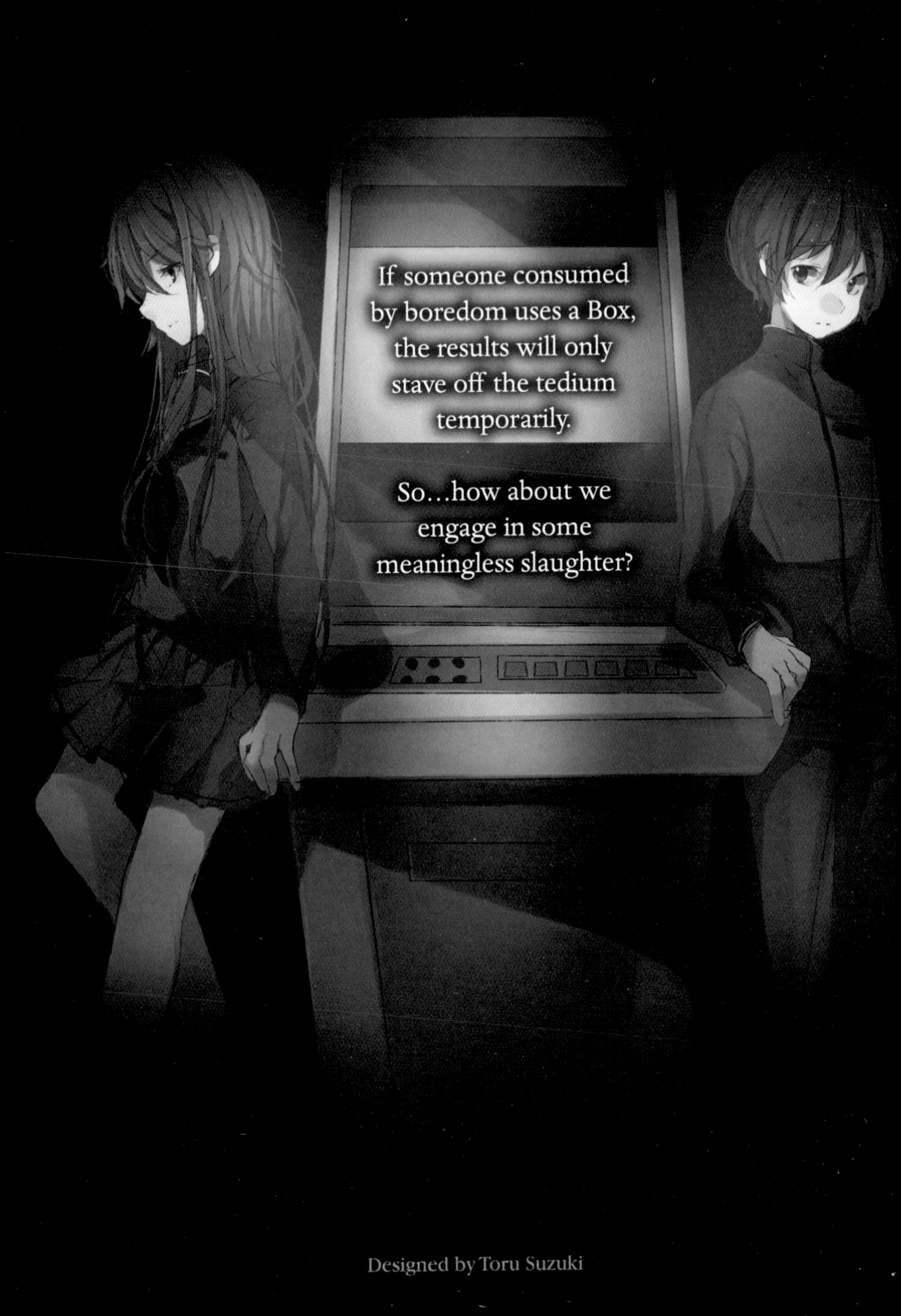

If someone consumed by boredom uses a Box, the results will only stave off the tedium temporarily.
So...how about we engage in some meaningless slaughter?

Designed by Toru Suzuki

Eiji Mikage

Illustration by Tetsuo

New York

The Empty Box and Zeroth Maria, Vol. 3
Eiji Mikage

Translation by Luke Baker
Cover art by Tetsuo

Yen On
1290 Avenue of the Americas
New York, NY 10104

Visit us at yenpress.com
facebook.com/yenpress
twitter.com/yenpress
yenpress.tumblr.com
instagram.com/yenpress

First Yen On Edition: June 2018

Yen On is an imprint of Yen Press, LLC.
The Yen On name and logo are trademarks of Yen Press, LLC.

Library of Congress Cataloging-in-Publication Data
Names: Mikage, Eiji author. | 415, illustrator. |
Tetsuo (Illustrator), illustrator. | Baker, Luke, translator.
Title: The empty box and zeroth Maria / Eiji Mikage ; illustration by 415, Tetsuo ; translation by Luke Baker.
Other titles: Utsuro no Hako to Zero no Maria. English
Description: New York, NY : Yen On, 2017– | v. 1 illustration by 415 — vols. 2–7 illustration by Tetsuo.
Identifiers: LCCN 2017027929 | ISBN 9780316561105 (v. 1 : paperback) |
ISBN 9780316561112 (v. 2 : paperback) | ISBN 9780316561136 (v. 3 : paperback)
Subjects: | CYAC: Science fiction. | BISAC: FICTION / Science Fiction / General.
Classification: LCC PZ7.1.M553 Em 2017 | DDC [Fic]—dc23
LC record available at https://lccn.loc.gov/2017027929

ISBNs: 978-0-316-56113-6 (paperback)
978-0-316-56126-6 (ebook)

1 3 5 7 9 10 8 6 4 2

LSC-C

Printed in the United States of America

I'm in the midst of sights I can remember only in dreams.

I wonder how many times I've met him now (or is it her?)… I guess it doesn't matter.

As usual, I can't make heads or tails of what they're saying, so I decide to just let it go in one ear and out the other.

Still, one comment does reach me clearly.

"That's right. Daiya Oomine is your enemy."

The first time I laid eyes on that silver hair, I never thought we would be a part of each other's lives at all.

I'm sure the majority of my classmates had the same first impression as I did. Everything about Daiya Oomine was a rejection of others, and his overbearing attitude and tendency to dress like a rocker were a means of distancing himself from the rest of us.

But we became friends. Haruaki was a major part of it as the go-between, but that alone isn't enough to really connect with someone.

"Uh…Kazuki Hoshino, right? I can't put my finger on it, but there's something strange about you."

That was the first thing Daiya ever said to me. Even so, I believed he meant to be friendly, and I could always tell he really enjoyed talking with me.

But then he had to say what he did.

"You're mixed up with O, aren't you?"

We're on our lunch break right before midterms, and he's sitting casually next to Maria in the cafeteria when he drops the bombshell.

"……Daiya, have you received a Box?" Maria asks the question for me, as I'm too stunned to speak.

"Clearly, I don't need to answer, so why are you even asking? Of course I have. And I'm talking to Kazu here. His mom can shut up and butt out."

Maria lets out a dramatic sigh and falls quiet, giving me a look as if to say he's all mine to deal with now.

What exactly does she expect me to say, though…?

Daiya takes the lead, ignoring me as I simply stare at him, unable to respond.

"I always knew something strange was going on. Otonashi showing up, you confessing to Kokone, not to mention all the other stuff."

Daiya touches one of the earrings in his right ear.

"Then I met O, and it all became clear. It happened in that moment. It was like, 'Oh, so this freak—for lack of a better word—is responsible for all the crap that's been happening recently. And then O told me about their interest in you."

I continue to sit quietly and listen, unsure of what Daiya is getting at.

"I realized I wasn't the only one who found something off about you… You see, Kazu, after a year of observation, I've figured out something about you."

Daiya fixes me with a piercing gaze as he continues:

"It's like you're floating, somehow."

"Floating…?"

The word makes no sense in context, so it takes me a moment to realize I haven't misheard.

"It's like you're watching us all from somewhere slightly above. You are where you are, but deep down, you're maintaining a certain distance. You're not part of the group or outside of it; you're just…above it."

I frown, unable to parse his meaning.

"And yet, you still cling to your everyday life. I used to have no idea why you'd want to keep things normal, but when I spoke with O…I learned you refused one of those wish-granting Boxes, and I finally understood."

Daiya speaks forcefully:

"Your goal is to crush other people's wishes."

"That's not true!"

I'm surprised at how loud my voice is. Still, this is where I draw the line.

"The reason I care so much about normalcy…is because I believe searching for something is proof you're alive. That's why…"

"Don't make me laugh."

So he says, but his eyes and mouth aren't so much as smiling.

"If that's true, then are you seeking something yourself? Answer me."

"Of course I am. It's..."

I stop short.

I am. I have to be. But for some reason, I can't say it.

...I'm sure it still hasn't properly formulated in my mind, and that's why.

"It's because you want to keep seeking. Hmph, even if I accept what you're saying for the sake of argument, that still brings up another question. *Why have you become like that?*"

"...Huh?"

Why am I so obsessed with maintaining normalcy in my life?

Actually, now that he mentions it, have I always been this way? ...I don't think I have. So when did I...?

"......"

Something surfaces in my mind.

...It's a person, but I can't tell who they are through the haze.

I don't know who that blurry form belongs to. *I don't? ...No, if I'm being honest, I would recognize that silhouette through all the fog in the world, wouldn't I?*

Hers...

"Do you get it now?"

Daiya interrupts my thoughts, and the one I was beginning to see vanishes back into the mist.

"...Get what...?"

"No matter what reason you try to assign to it, you're just clinging to normalcy because you've been conditioned, like Pavlov's dog."

All I care about is keeping my life normal? If so, then...

"It's the same impulse that makes you walk all over other people's wishes... Listen, Kazu."

Daiya says my name as casually as he always does.

"I have a Box. Now I'm in opposition to your everyday life. What are you gonna do?"

I have no idea what Daiya's wish might be. But if it's going to throw my life into chaos, then I...

"You know the answer, right?"

Daiya lightly touches the earrings in his right ear as he emotionlessly makes his position clear.

"That means...I'm your enemy."

✦

Our term-end tests have already come back, so we're focusing on our July classes about as well as we would on a throwaway match in a tournament.

"Okay, while we're at the hospital, don't you say a word about going to the mall later!" Kokone says as we make our way to Mogi's hospital room. She's been wearing her hair in a bun lately. "That goes double for you, Haruaki!"

"I know that."

"Oh really? I heard people have been using this new word 'Haruaki' that means 'oblivious.'"

"Never heard of it! The only new word I know is 'KK,' which means 'shut up.'"

"Hey! Why do my initials mean 'shut up'?!"

"Kirino, if Mogi overhears you shouting, your thoughtfulness will go to waste," Maria points out.

"Tee-hee," Kokone giggles, then winks and sticks out her tongue.

"Is that supposed to be cute?" Haruaki mutters, earning him a glare from her.

This is par for the course between those two, and I sigh before entering the hospital room.

"..."

I'm greeted by the sight of a magazine with a shirtless macho man on the cover.

"Kasumi...?"

"Huh...? Eep!" She quickly shoves the magazine under a blanket. "H-hey, everyone... Wh-what's up? You're earlier than usual today..." An awkward smile appears on her face.

"......"

Maybe we saw something we shouldn't have...? Kokone and I give each other a look of silent agreement: *Let's not even touch this one.*

"Hey, what've you got hidden there, Kasumi?"

But it's no use. We have Mr. Oblivious with us.

"I-I'm not hiding anything..."

"You can't lie to me... Hmm, maybe it's a porno mag? Show me, show me! I've always wanted to know what kind of porn gets girls— Oof!"

Kokone gives Haruaki a sharp jab with her elbow. Yeah, that was the right way to shut him up.

"Don't worry, Kasumi. We didn't see anything. Mm-hmm... I mean, you've been stuck here in the hospital all this time, and...yeah. Things get a little pent up, right?"

"N-n-n-nothing is getting pent up!!"

Her face bright red, Mogi waves her arms in denial.

"Th-that's not what this is at all! It's...well..."

She purses her lips and hesitates for a moment before pulling the magazine back out from under the blanket. On closer inspection, I can see that despite the buff model on the cover, the contents are actually about yoga, proper physical training techniques, and similar topics.

"It's a magazine with exercises in it. It's not...porny."

"Huh? Hey, she's right. Ah-ha-ha, sorry 'bout that! ...But why did you hide it?"

For some reason Mogi looks at me and not Kokone as she softly replies, "...I mean, it looks a little strange for me to be reading it..."

Now that she mentions it, I instinctively glance at Mogi's arms. Her pale limbs used to seem so ready to break, but now they're a bit sturdier... Still delicate, though.

Following my gaze, Mogi seems embarrassed for some reason and hides her arms behind her back. "...I thought it might help out a bit with rehab," she explains.

It's already been four months since the endless repetition came to an end. Mogi's broken bones have mended, and she's begun the rehabilitation process. Her return to school, once such a distant dream, is now that much closer to becoming reality. Before too long, Mogi and her wheelchair will become a fixture in the classroom.

She'll be a part of my normal daily life again.

...Just like when Maria wasn't.

"Hey, Maria, do you not like Kasumi or something?" Haruaki asks the moment we step into the shopping mall. It's something both Kokone and I have wondered, but we've never been able to actually voice our concern...

"Haru... You scare me sometimes...," Kokone says.

"Why?"

Haruaki can't even read between the lines. He really is frightening.

"...Why do you think I don't like her?" Maria asks Haruaki with a casual lack of emotion.

"It's just that I've never seen you and Kasumi actually talking to each other before, you know? I mean, it could be because I've never seen you two together without anyone else around, either."

"...Listen up, Haru." Kokone pulls Haruaki toward her and whispers into his ear. "...They're rivals in love... That's why things are weird between them. I'm sure you get *that*, at least..."

Um, Kokone...? I know you're trying to be thoughtful, but we can hear everything you're saying.

Haruaki is staring at me with a grin on his face... Man, he really knows how to get under my skin.

Maria lets out a sigh at their antics. "You're free to interpret things however you want, but if the question is whether I find it easy to talk to her, the answer is no."

"Whoo, do I smell a rivalry after all?"

"Usui, if someone were to treat you like an insect and then plunge a knife into your stomach, would you be able to talk to them without anything weighing on your mind?"

"Pardon?"

"I'm joking."

Haruaki and Kokone look at each other in response to Maria's deadpan question.

...Guess I'm the only one whose heart is aching from her near revelation.

"...Anyway, that's enough of that... Now it's time for the main event: finding some clothes that look nice on Maria! You'll probably be fine no matter what you wear, though... Damn you and that model figure of yours!"

Says the girl featured in a fashion magazine the other day.

"Wait, so what does that have to do with any of this?"

"Just listen and you'll find out! On our days off lately, I've been bumping into Maria in her street clothes more often, and she's obviously completely neglecting her fashion. It's not that her sense is bad, just that there's no personal flair... And when I asked what brand she wears, she said UNIQLO."

"Maybe it wasn't always that way, but UNIQLO is in right now. The company has invested considerable effort into selling a wide range of high-quality products that are also low priced. They are superior."

"I wear UNIQLO, too! But that's not what I'm getting at! It's just that I put more...I don't know...effort into being my ideal version of myself... Agh, I've had it! I can still compete with you when it comes to this, dammit!!"

"Don't worry, Kiri. You have her beat in the chest department, if nothing else."

"If nothing else?! Quit being stupid, Haru! ...Big boobs aren't the only thing I..."

Kokone's words fade as she carefully looks Maria over from head to toe with dismay.

"...Come on... Don't tell me there's no way I can win! Waaah, what the hell?! You'd better become Miss whatever-it's-called, the prettiest in the world! Then I can acknowledge that you're beautiful without feeling bad about myself!"

"...K-Kokone, beauty is in the eye of the beholder, you know..."

"Okay then, Kazu, which one of us do you think is better looking?"

"......"

"Why aren't you saying anything?! Even if it's a lie, you have to say me!"

"That's a tall order for him," Haruaki commented.

"Shut up, you barely qualify for average!"

"What?! I am *above* average, and that's putting it mildly!"

Thanks to their yammering, we're beginning to attract the attention of the other customers around us... This always happens when Kokone's around.

"H-hey, Kokone, don't you think it's about time you...?"

Kokone stares me down after I speak up. Oh man, I'm about to get tangled up in this, aren't I...?

"Hey, Kazu, you wanna know what I really can't stand about Mari-Mari's wardrobe? It's that you two are almost exactly the same height and share clothes!"

"...Huh? Is that bad?"

Kokone's eyes go wide at my words. "...The heck? Why do you look so shocked? Don't go saying '...Huh? Is that bad?'! Your sensibilities are out of whack! I almost passed out when I saw you and Mari-Mari wearing the same T-shirt on different days, you know!"

I really don't get what the problem is, so I look over at Haruaki.

"Nah, she's right, man."

...He shut me down, too.

"You know what you are? You're one of those guys who doesn't think twice about downing the rest of a bottle when the girl he likes can't finish it, aren't you?"

"Isn't that normal...?"

As if to demonstrate his point, Haruaki flings his hands toward the sky in exasperation and lets out a sigh.

...Hey, what was that for?

"Now do you see why I'm trying to get her to buy clothes, Haru?"

"All too well!"

Now that those two have joined forces, the selection of clothes for Maria begins according to Kokone's plan. Still, Maria herself seems to have little to no interest in shopping, so she just offers comments on the options Kokone throws at her and occasionally tries them on under duress.

As I watch, I wonder if Kokone must be unhappy because Maria isn't buying any of her suggestions, but she actually seems to be enjoying herself. In her words: "I have an unparalleled beauty as my doll for playing dress-up, and that's fun enough!" ...As a guy, I can't say I relate.

As for my fellow man Haruaki, he seems to be content ogling the female customers and staff at the shops. I kind of envy the way his mind works... Actually, I don't. I don't at all.

Standing there by myself, I suggest taking a breather to Kokone, who has been going full throttle this entire time. I have no idea where she gets her energy. Three hours later, she eventually accepts.

Phew... I'm finally free, at least for the moment.

"...You seem like you're having a good time, Haruaki!"

"You know it! I spent my time ranking all the girls I saw, so I feel like I got something done! The top of the list was one of the girls working at the last store," he replies.

Kokone is not amused.

"She kinda looked like our student council president. Didn't you think so, Hosshi?"

"...Well, now that you mention it, I guess she did, a little bit."

"Hmm... Are you sure?" counters Kokone. "Our president is way cooler in my book… Hey, that reminds me—have you heard of the 'Superhuman Three'?"

"Of course I have," Haruaki says.

"…Well, I have encountered the term," Maria adds.

It seems like the only one who hasn't is me.

"…Who are these 'Superhuman Three'?"

"Okay, so in our school, there's one student in each year who has amazing scores, right? Well, as you can imagine, all three of them have something special beyond just their grades, so someone started referring to them as superhumans. The label fit so well that eventually everyone in the school started using it."

"…And I'm guessing Maria is one of them?"

"Yes. I don't really care what people say about me, but I don't relish being the center of attention."

Uh…you're saying that after the stunt at the entrance ceremony?

"So, if the first-year is Maria, and the third-year is the president, then the second-year superhuman is…" Kokone stops on the verge of saying the name and becomes visibly upset.

…So the last one must be Daiya.

Daiya had vanished without a trace after announcing he was a Box owner to me that day in the cafeteria. He hadn't come to school, and he wasn't at home, either.

He hadn't said a word to Kokone or Haruaki.

Kokone is furious about the entire thing. She can't believe he would just up and leave without telling her. Of course, it's just a roundabout way of expressing her concern.

Kokone probably believes Daiya's absence is temporary. That's why she can be angry about it. But as for me…I can't help but think this might be more permanent.

I mean…he did receive a Box, after all. He removed himself from our everyday lives.

Still scowling, Kokone drains the rest of her caramel macchiato in one go with a little *phew* before continuing, "I couldn't care less about that asshole, but the point is that the Superhuman Three are unusual, no matter how you slice it."

"I can see what you mean about Maria and Daiya… Is the president incredible, too?"

"She is. They say her grades are good enough to get her into Tokyo University no sweat, she goes to national tournaments for her sprinting and long jump in the track club, and she's even modernizing school regulations as part of the student council. But apparently, it's also easy to see why she's amazing even if you don't know any of that superficial stuff."

"…What do you mean?"

"This is just the story I heard, but the president isn't a superfast sprinter during practice. She even gets beat by other members of the team sometimes. When it's the real deal, though, she always wins and gets a new best time."

"So she slacks off during practice?"

"No, no, no. To her, the goal of practice is to expand her potential. The goal of actual matches is to get results. That's why it makes sense that she would be at her fastest during matches, where all the weight is placed on displaying her abilities to the fullest. According to her anyway… You see? I don't really get it all, but it's still awesome, right?"

"…Yeah. Sounds like she's from another dimension."

"Right?" Kokone quickly checks to make sure our drinks are finished, then smirks. "Okay! It's about time we got back to dressing up Maria!"

Ugh, I honestly don't know if I can stand any more waiting around…

"K-Kokone, I have to make it home in time for dinner, so I'd better be going…"

"Whaaaat…?" Kokone pouts. "Just one more shop! They have some clothes I absolutely have to see Maria in!"

The next place Kokone leads us to gives off a strange vibe even before we go in. Pretty much all the clothes are black and oddly frilly.

"I just know this'll be perfect for you! You'll be little goth-loli Maria, ha-ha!"

The overly excited Kokone holds up a tacky black dress with tons of frills. Maria's face understandably twitches a bit as she accepts the garment. "…And I'm supposed to wear this?"

"Yep! …By the way, what do you think of gothic Lolita fashion, Mari-Mari?"

"It doesn't feel grounded in reality."

"Then it's perfect for you!"

Yikes! K-kinda dropped a bomb there, don't you think…?!

I look over at Maria fearfully. Fortunately, she seems more concerned with the dress Kokone forced into her hands than the comment.

"Now we need a headdress… Or maybe one of those miniature hats!" Kokone says, rummaging through the accessories.

Maria sighs.

"…If you really don't like it, then you should just say no," I offer.

Maria looks between the goth-loli dress and me as she asks, "Do you want to see me wear it, too?"

"Huh?"

"I'm asking if you want to see me in this."

I don't know exactly what she's getting at, so I answer honestly. "…Well, if I had to say one way or the other, I would say I do."

"I see. If it means that much to you, I'll try it on."

"…Hey, it doesn't mean *that* much…"

"I'm only going to wear this because you said I should. You really are hopeless."

……Okay?

Wait, does Maria actually want to try it out herself?

And thus, goth-loli Maria arrived.

"Ohhhhh myyyy gooooooood! Mari-Mari, step on me! Just…step on me!!"

Whoa, what do I do? She broke Kokone…

"My selection was too perfect. Don't you agree, Kazu?!"

"Y-yeah."

The style definitely suits her, no doubt about that. Haruaki is over there nodding with a satisfied expression, and even the staff here are peeking into the changing area. That's how good it looks.

Maria, meanwhile, is staring at nothing in particular with her arms crossed, apparently unsure how to react.

"Hey, Kazu, is that it?"

"…Is what it?"

"I dunno… Shouldn't you be acting more impressed? Y'know, gaping like some idiot as you unknowingly mumble, 'S-so beautiful…,' and then Mari-Mari overhears you and gets embarrassed, so she acts tough to try to cover her blushing, like, 'Hmph, so you like me when I'm dressed like this?' and then you're suddenly all like, 'N-no, you're always beautiful in my mind! You're gorgeous,' and then you and Mari-Mari are both just standing there, sheepishly blushing like some cheap sappy drama. And then I punch you."

"......No."

"You're so boring. You're the type of guy who goes to karaoke and only sings ballads nobody else knows. Even worse, you're not really good or bad at it, so no one has anything to say about your singing... Whatever, Kazu, you don't matter. Hey, Mari-Mari, can I take a picture?"

"Absolutely not."

Maria's gaze flicks away as she says this, her arms still crossed.

...Wait. Don't tell me she really is embarrassed dressing like this?

"What're you smiling about, Kazuki?"

"Huh?"

"You were leering at me. It would appear the real reason you wanted me to try this on was to humiliate me."

"Th-that's not the case at all..."

"Come here."

I step in front of Maria, ducking in anticipation of her anger. Goth-loli Maria assumes a commanding pose, her arms folded.

"Does it suit me?"

Wondering why she's asking me this, I nod quickly.

"I see."

Maria removes the lacy white headdress. Looking at the accessory in her hands, the corners of her mouth turn in a smile. And then...

"...Huh?"

...for some reason, she plunks it on my head.

"Hmm, it suits you, too."

"...What?"

The look on Maria's face is pure delight.

"I only tried on this getup because you claimed you absolutely had to see me in it. Isn't that right?"

"...Um?"

"Isn't that right?"

"...Yes."

"I listened to one selfish request from you, so now it's your turn to humor me, right?"

"...Sure, I guess."

"This fits me perfectly. You and I wear the same size, so that means it'll fit you, too."

"......"

Maria brooks no discussion as she tells me:

"Put it on."

And that's how I became a gothic Lolita.

"Ugh..."

I groan at the awful sight of myself in the changing room.

I'm sure Maria only wore this because she intended to get it on me from the very beginning. She was cornering me so I couldn't refuse. Now that I think about it, she was looking back and forth between me and the dress when she was holding it.

"Hey, you should be dressed by now, Kazuki. Hurry up and open the door."

"Maria. Why did you do this to me...?"

"Because I absolutely have to see you in goth-loli getup, why else? And of course because I wanted to see you embarrassed, too."

Maria hasn't bullied me like this in a while...!

Well, I can't stay holed up in the changing room forever. I steel myself and open the door.

"Gah-ha-ha-ha-ha-ha!"

Kokone immediately points and laughs. I would be okay if Kokone, Maria, and Haruaki were the only ones out front, but for some reason the staff and even a few nosy shoppers are there, too. What is this, a public execution...?

"Gah-ha-ha-ha, you're adorable, Kazuki!" Kokone crows, whipping out her cell phone and turning it toward me... *She can't be serious.*

"S-stop! Don't take pictures of me!"

"Sorry. I have to."

And it's not just Kokone. Haruaki and even Maria are snapping away. And after she didn't let anyone take pictures of her, too! Now even the customers who don't know me are getting in on it!

"Don't worry, Kazu. You look very cute," Maria adds. I'm not sure how to take that.

"Now then, time to send it."

"H-hold on, Kokone, wh-who are you sending it to?"

"Huh? Kasumi, who else!"

"Wh-what do you think you're doing?! I thought you said it would be better if we didn't tell her we were going to the mall!"

"Are you dumb or something, Kazu? There are such things as priorities in the world, you know."

You're the one who's stupid, Kokone! This is too low!

...My phone begins to vibrate almost immediately. I open it fearfully. I have one new message, and the sender's name is *Kasumi Mogi.*

The message consists of only a single line.

Cute. ♡

Screw it, I don't care. ☆

I wake up to a stench pungent enough to give me a headache.

"Huh...?"

A gasp of surprise at this sudden turn of events slips past my lips. The last thing I remember is diving into bed hoping to forget the potentially lifelong trauma of what happened today. I probably fell asleep after that...

...But then, where am I?

It's black and dark. The air is thick with desire, like someone put it in a pot and boiled it down into a syrup. The atmosphere is sticky and sultry, clinging to my body. Viscous and gluey—over all of me.

Hesitantly, I get to my feet.

The view filling my eyes is all black, black, black, looming close and threatening to overwhelm me. I fight off the urge to collapse by planting a foot forward.

I notice a faint light within the darkness—a weak, pallid flickering. It's like those electric bug zappers they have out in front of convenience stores. Even though I know it's the last thing I should do, I find myself compelled to approach.

It seems to be about five yards away. Even so, each time I take a step forward, it feels like it's getting that much farther away. My senses are ignoring reality and drawing out the distance.

Squish…

My foot hits something. I look down.

"……Ack!"

It's a girl's body.

"Uh—ah, aah! Haah, haah, haaaaah…" As I struggle to get my breathing back under control, I look down at her again. She's a young girl I don't know with long hair, wearing pajamas… Wait, maybe I have at least seen her somewhere before. Maybe just enough to be somewhere in my memory…?

She's not breathing. But she's not dead, either. It's more like she's just… stopped.

I check my own clothes. I'm dressed the same way I was when I went to bed, in the T-shirt and shorts I use instead of pajamas.

I think I get it now. This girl and I were probably brought here while we were asleep.

And this…*must be the inside of that Box.*

I finally arrive directly in front of that pale light. Upon closer inspection, I see it's coming from the cabinet of an old arcade game like the ones you'd find at a run-down hot-spring inn. On the display is what appears to be the title screen for something called *Kingdom Royale.*

I spot someone standing next to the game cabinet.

"……Daiya."

He's no different from before he disappeared, piercings and all.

"Long time no see, Kazu. What's it been, two months or so?"

He's speaking like we're about to have a normal little chat. I have plenty to say to him, but first I ask the obvious question.

"…Is this your Box?"

"Do I really need to answer?" He's right. It goes without saying that Daiya has finally used his Box. "Tedium is a monster… Some people might even try to slay it with a bullet to their own brains."

I frown, unable to parse his comment.

He smiles and clarifies. "It's a line from the book *Hatachi no etude.*"

"…What's all this about, Daiya?"

"The wish I made with this Box, the 'Game of Indolence.'"

I still have no idea what he's getting at.

"You're confused, I guess. Someone who enjoys mundanity like you probably doesn't even have the capacity for boredom. Well, let me tell you, it's a source of unimaginable pain and suffering."

Is Daiya saying he dragged us in here for the Game of Indolence because he was bored? If so, it doesn't get much more selfish than that, not to mention ridiculous.

"Judging by your face, I'm guessing you're unwilling to try to understand me. People without imagination are always full of themselves."

"......You can't fool me. Using a Box to relieve your boredom is just stupid."

"That's fine if you don't care to listen. Just remember, some people out there do feel that way."

"...Well, maybe they should change that."

"That's not possible. It's an issue with their core as a person. You can't just rewrite someone's true nature."

"That's...an excuse."

"All right, then how about you correct your twisted obsession with normal life, too?"

I shut my mouth.

"No matter what you do, no matter where you go, there's no escaping who you are inside. Just like how an ugly person will always be ugly no matter how expensive their clothes are or how much time they spend on makeup. You can't change something immutable."

"...So boredom is unbearable for you, but why does it have to be that way? There's lots to enjoy out there, you know?"

"That's just the way your core nature works. It catches and alters everything that happens. Things you find enjoyable will just be tedious to someone who's naturally bored."

"...And yet, here we all are, jealous of you and your abilities."

"I'm nothing special. I know because I can see the limits of my own faculties. I will never accomplish anything and never obtain anything. I realize that now."

I'm shocked at the bluntness of his admission. I never would have imagined someone like Daiya, who always seems so sure of himself, could think this way.

"If someone consumed by boredom uses a Box, the results will only stave off the tedium temporarily. That's why this is all just a diversion. A pointless game." Daiya's mouth twitches up in a smile. "All the same, it's still very important to me."

I can't seem to make heads or tails of his logic. But I'm now well aware that I'm never getting through to him with words.

"...Hey, Daiya. What kind of Box is this anyway?"

Daiya smiles faintly, then grips me by the shoulders and pushes me down onto the seat in front of the arcade machine.

"It's just a little game for warding off ennui. There's no meaning beyond that. So..."

Still maintaining a firm grip on my shoulders, Daiya leans in and whispers into my ear.

"...how about we engage in some meaningless slaughter?"

"...Huh?"

Daiya's thumbs have dug in under my collarbone so I can't escape. The screen in front of me begins to waver and sway. It's like I'm drunk.

...Squeeze.

In the midst of the intoxication, *something* grips my head.

Something is reaching out from the screen of the arcade machine. It's a transparent hand. And it has ahold of me.

"U-ungh..."

The inside of my head is crackling. More and more see-through hands appear. More, still more. The new limbs seize my head, my arms, my legs, my stomach, all of me, until my entire body is covered in them.

"D-Daiya—!!"

Daiya coolly ignores my angry glare, then says:

"See ya."

And that's when the hands...*drag me in.*

KAZUKI HOSHINO

MARIA OTONASHI

IROHA SHINDO

YURI YANAGI

KOUDAI KAMIUCHI

DAIYA OOMINE

START GAME

▶Day 1 <A> Kazuki Hoshino's Room

I wake up with a start in unfamiliar surroundings, and my eyes fall upon a naked light bulb and a bare concrete ceiling.

"...What is this room?"

I can feel myself about to lose it, so I review what I can remember of what happened.

I'm sure I was sleeping on my bottom bunk. I don't remember moving from there. *I don't remember leaving or meeting anyone, either.*

I look around the room. The space is about the size of six tatami mats with an exposed toilet and sink. There's also a table in the center of the room with a hemp sack lying on top of it.

What sticks out the most, however, is the cutting-edge twenty-inch monitor embedded in the wall, completely unbefitting this cell-like chamber.

I suddenly lower my gaze. I'm dressed in my school uniform with nothing in my pockets.

I reach into the hemp sack on the table and pull out its contents one at a time.

A pen. A notepad. A blue digital wristwatch. Seven sets of solid rations. A portable device that looks exactly like an iPod Touch.

And then...

"......"

...a knife, with a solid heft to it.

I slowly pull off the cover. The blade is thick, and it even has a serrated edge. It's an authentic combat knife, just like the ones the military guys use in the movies.

"...What the—? Why is this here...?"

It's clearly a weapon. An implement of warfare.

Is someone trying to make me fight? Or to put it another way, do I have to fight?

With a shake of my head, I toss the knife back in the bag. Realizing my body is trembling, I take a breath and try to collect myself.

I survey the room again. No windows. I can't spot any vents, either. There is a single, extremely heavy-looking door. I think about opening it, but then I notice there's no doorknob. I try pushing against it lightly, but it doesn't even budge.

I totter unsteadily toward the bed and plop down.

"What the hell is happening...?"

I don't understand. I don't understand...but this is not normal.

...It's not normal—not my everyday life.

I see. So maybe it's...

"Good_morning."

My heart almost leaps from my chest at the sudden voice.

I swivel my head, and on the previously black monitor I spot... What even is that? It's bizarre, whatever it is.

"Geh-heh-heh_good_morning_Kazuki."

Though the greeting itself is friendly, the voice sounds purely mechanical and devoid of intonation.

On the monitor is a lurid primary-green...bear, I think—maybe. The creature's eyes have a sharp glint, and its overall misshapen form isn't cute in the slightest—pretty gross, honestly.

"HeY_hey_hey_how_are_you? I_am_the_mascot_Noitan. Nice_to_meet_YoU."

The mouth of the bear (Noitan?) moves up and down, although all the sprite is doing is raising and lowering its chin. Like I said, creepy.

"...What a horrible character. This would scare any kid to tears..."

"Who the hell are you calling horrible, you pig? You want me to smash your balls and make you a eunuch? Not that it wouldn't suit you."

"......Eep!"

H-he spoke back to me! And not only that, but he's incredibly vulgar and really fluent all of a sudden!

Those wide-open, bloodshot eyes are terrifying, too!

"...U-uh...can you speak to me?"

"YeaH_I_can."

The weird inflection is back. I guess he's designed to only speak smoothly when he's angry.

"Noitan—"

"That's 'Mr. Noitan' to you, you presumptuous sack of trash. Be polite."

"......Mr. Noitan. I don't know how I got here. Could you tell me where I am?"

"Inside_a_game_called_*Kingdom_Royale*. I'll_exPLain_moRE_later_when_EVEryone_has_gathered_but—"

"Everyone...? You mean I'm not the only one here?!"

"Okay, asshole, if you don't learn to let people finish before butting in, I'll rip out your tongue."

"......I'm sorry."

"The_door_is_going_to_open. Outside_you_wILL_find_the_other_PLAyers_in_the_gaMe. I_will_EXplain_more_theRE_so_WAIt_a_bit_okay?" Noitan says, and the heavy door slowly but smoothly begins to open.

"...May I leave?"

"You_CAn_whEN_you_are_ready."

"Ready...?"

"Outside_the_door_Is_a_cOmmON_rOom. There_you_will_find_PEoPle_iN_the_saMe_poSItion_as_yoU. Are_you_reaDY_to_meeT_those_people?"

"And what are we supposed to do?"

Noitan's face contorts into that disturbing sprite.

"Kill one another," he says.

"......Huh? What the—?"

Before I can finish speaking, the monitor shuts off. The door fully opens at exactly the same moment.

What is that?

An inky-black darkness like desire laid bare leads out from beyond the door.

So there's a room out there? ...I find that hard to believe. I'm pretty sure refusing to go isn't an option, though.

I put on the blue wristwatch lying on the table and stand in front the door. I try to talk myself down as the terror threatens to overwhelm me.

...You'll be fine. Everything's gonna be okay.

I know nothing good lies ahead. But this is the inside of a Box, so she'll be here.

...Maria will be here.

That's how I know I'll be okay.

And with that, I plunge forward into the darkness.

▶Day 1 <B> The Common Area

The view changes instantly.

The first thing I notice is that it's white. Unnaturally so, like a newly built hospital without doctors or nurses or patients.

I have just enough time to take it in, and then...

"Urgh...?"

...I'm knocked flat.

Before I have time to wonder what happened or even register the pain of slamming against the floor, I'm staring down the point of a knife.

"What's your name?"

I finally process the situation as I see a girl with midlength hair holding the weapon out at me.

"A-ahh..."

"Your name is 'Ahh'? I'm guessing no. I want you to tell me your name here."

Wh-who is this person?

"K-Kazuki Hoshino."

I notice she's wearing a uniform from my school and has an orange digital watch on her left wrist. Unsurprisingly, it's the same as the watch I'm wearing, just a different color.

Does that mean she's another player in the game? ...Huh? Wait, has the killing already started, and this is checkmate for me? H-hold up, this is unfair!

Just as the situation looked to be too much...

★ ★ ★

"Kazuki!"

...Yeah, just hearing that voice makes me feel a million times better.

"Hmm, do you know him, Otonashi?"

"Yes, I do."

The girl with the longish hair returns her gaze to me for a closer examination.

"...Hmm," she says. She stands up, her expression never changing, and moves away. I don't really get what happened, but apparently, she's let me go.

"Are you all right, Kazuki?" Maria comes running up.

"Y-yeah..." I answer as I grab her extended hand. "B-but why exactly did she...?"

"Whoa!"

At the sound of yet another voice, I stop short and turn around to see what's happening. The same girl has turned her knife on a boy with brown hair.

"...What's this all about?" he asks as his eyes move to take in his surroundings. He seems surprised, but he's also calm enough to be curious about us.

"...You're awfully relaxed," the girl comments, noticing the brown-haired boy's attitude.

"Nah, that's not true... I guess once I saw in your eyes that you weren't going to go through with it, I knew I'd probably be okay."

The girl answers him with a meaningful "Huh." She then withdraws her knife and lets him go.

"...Oh, is that it?"

"Yes, go ahead."

...She backed off from the brown-haired guy just like that, too. *Why does she keep doing that?*

Now that he's off the hook, the brunet acts like he's completely forgotten what just happened to him. "Oh-ho, three young beauties. Today's my lucky day," he says with a carefree smile.

Three...? Let's see, there's Maria, the girl with the knife, and then...

Next to the big monitor in the room, I spot a girl with long hair curled up in a small ball, as if trying to hug herself. Her skin is pale, striking a contrast with her deep-black hair that gives her a very trim and neat appearance.

And then there's the beige watch around her wrist.

"It's okay, Yuri!"

With a kindness not shown to us, the knife girl smiles and pats the black-haired girl on the head. The other girl's fearful face relaxes slightly, but the darkness soon returns to her expression.

"...What's going to happen to us?"

"We'll figure something out!"

...Guess those two know each other.

"You're *the* Kazuki Hoshino, correct?"

I look away from the two girls and toward the one who spoke to me. It's the guy with brown hair.

"Do you know me?"

"Of course I do. Everybody knows you and Maricchi are a set. Don't tell me you forgot about that epic entrance ceremony."

As he answers, I notice his worn-out school uniform, silver necklace, and green digital watch on his arm... *Now that I think about it, everyone here is dressed as a student from our school.*

"Um, so what's your name?"

"I'm— Oh yeah. Hey, President, it seems like the gang's all here, so how about we do a round of self-introductions?" he says to the knife girl.

President? Does he mean the student council president? One of the Superhuman Three Kokone was talking about?

"You're right. That might be a good idea."

Now that I think about it, I've heard this same clear articulation through a microphone many times before. This girl with her confident smile... Yeah, no doubt about it—she's the president of the student council.

So that means...I'm supposed to lock horns with a superhuman in a game of kill or be killed?

"Is this everyone?" the president asks the brunet.

"There're chairs for six, so I'd think so."

"Yeah, you're probably right."

...Huh? Six?

"Hold on a minute, there's only five of us here—"

"Kazu, you got eyes in that head of yours?"

I hold my breath.

The six chairs are arranged evenly around the rectangular table in the middle of the room, and he's sitting in the farthest one from me.

"...Daiya."

Dressed in his school uniform, Daiya's lips curl up in a little smile, and he raises his arm with its black digital watch as if to say, *Long time no see.*

We haven't seen each other in two months, we're finally meeting again in a place like this, and yet he's greeting me like it's been hardly any time at all.

"What? You know each other, too? ......I see."

"President. Does that mean you're nervous about us joining forces?"

For just a moment, the president seems caught off guard, but then she sighs and says, "Do whatever you want."

This time, Daiya smirks.

What was up with that little interaction...? It's like they're already squaring off for battle... Or maybe it's already begun? Is that why she pulled the knife on me?

"So I'm the one without any friends here? Being the odd man out sucks!"

The brown-haired kid clutches his head dramatically as if completely unaware of the tension between the two... *Given his behavior, I wonder if he has any idea what's happening to him...?*

"Okay, right, self-introductions," the president says. "Shall we give that a try? Let's have a seat in these chairs since they've set them up for us."

I sit directly across from Daiya, and Maria sits next to me. As I thought, there's a watch on her wrist, too. It's red.

"Now then, I'm sure you might already know a bit about me, but I'll go ahead and start. I'm—"

"Can I say something first?" Maria interrupts, glaring at the student council president across from her.

"What?"

"I didn't stop you earlier because I didn't get the feeling you were really going to hurt him, but...what was the point of threatening Kazuki?"

"Oh, that?" The president explains, completely unfazed by the angry gaze directed her way. "If that ridiculous bear told you the same things it told me, then everyone already knows we're about to play a game of killing. Right? That being the case, I figured someone might try to get a head start while everyone was confused, and if I did what I did, it might deter them. So in essence, I was just doing a bit of risk management."

"Heh." Daiya snorts derisively at that explanation.

The president is openly upset. "Okay... I'm pretty sure you're Daiya Oomine. I've heard rumors about you. What was that sneer for?"

"Oh, just thinking that was an awful lie. Risk management? Do you really think anyone here is bloodthirsty enough to try to kill everyone because of that bear? It was all your plan to get the drop on us and establish a mental advantage, right? Don't worry; the only one who would pull that is someone who's already considering the possibility, like you."

"A plan to gain a mental edge, eh? Wrong, so, so wrong. I'd never go for a plan with so many disadvantages. That'd just get me on everyone's bad side, maybe even make me a target."

"So you were just trying to find the mastermind? Gauging everyone's reactions to see if you could catch someone behaving suspiciously?"

"Oh, stop, I wasn't thinking that far ahead." The president responds lightly, but I still can't shake the feeling that a storm is brewing.

"Come on now, you guys. You're all starting to freak me out here!" the brown-haired boy interjects.

"...Fine, but I have to say, you're taking this remarkably well. I can tell you're a tricky one," the president replies.

"Cut me some slack. This is just what I'm like when I'm feeling off. Normally, I'm pretty quiet, but now I'm just a bit worked up or something... I don't think I'm as nervous as your friend there, though."

The quiet girl's shoulders jerk as the conversation suddenly turns to her. "I-I'm sorry..."

"It's okay, Yuri. There's no need to apologize."

"S-sorry, Iroha."

The president smiles and shrugs at the girl apologizing next to her. "Ahh... I can just feel all the stress leaving me."

"Nice one, Yuri." The brown-haired boy gives her a thumbs-up.

"Huh? What? Did I do something...?"

The president starts giggling again as the girl blinks in confusion. "Shall we get back to the matter at hand and start those introductions? As you know, I'm Iroha Shindo, third-year student and the student council president. My skill is being able to fall asleep anywhere. My hobby is track and field."

"You're good enough at track and field to compete in national tournaments, and you call it a hobby? People must hate your guts," Daiya interrupts.

"Well, listen to you. But the simple truth is that it is just a hobby. I'm actually not cut out for track at all. You have to rely on your physical abilities. As it happens, I'm not especially gifted there, which is why I'm not cut out for it; thus, it's just a hobby."

"That's what I'm saying people hate about you."

"Says the hateful little boy," the president retorts without even missing a beat. She really is superhuman if she can go toe to toe with Daiya like this.

She nudges the girl next to her, prompting her to go next.

"Ah, I-I'm, um, a third-year, and, um, I've been one of Iroha's friends since we were in the same class during our first year... Um, do I really need to say my skills, Iroha? Um...I don't really know if I have any skills... but my hobby is reading. My name is Yuri... *Yuri Yanagi.*"

"Huh?" The word escapes my mouth before I can stop it. *Did she say Yanagi?*

"......Huh? Um, ah, did I say something strange?" The girl calling herself "Yuri Yanagi" seems flustered by my reaction.

"Ah." I get ahold of myself and wave my hands vigorously. "I-it's nothing. It's just...I have a friend with the same last name."

"O-oh, I see..."

Yanagi—no, that'll just confuse things, so Yuri—is still giving me a strange look.

"Are you through, Yuri?" the president asks.

"Oh, um..." Yuri looks away. "N-nice to meet you."

...Oh great, now she probably thinks I'm some sort of weirdo.

Having watched all this with a grin on his face, the brown-haired boy opens his mouth.

"You're a real cutie, Yuri, dear. Just my type."

"What?!"

"Hold on there, first-year. Don't go hitting on Yuri. Don't speak so familiarly to her, either."

"Just so you know, President, you're a bit too aggressive for my tastes."

"As if I care. You introduce yourself next."

"All righty. I'm Koudai Kamiuchi from first year, nice to meetcha. Oh, and it's especially nice to meet you, Yuri. So, my hobby is slot machines... Oh, the ones in arcades, I mean."

Daiya seems unexpectedly interested in Koudai Kamiuchi, the brown-haired boy, as he introduces himself. "Ahh, so you're Kamiuchi, huh? I've heard a lot about you. Apparently, you never lose at pachinko slots."

"Eh, that's not true. Well, I guess overall I probably having a winning record. I just have good eyes."

"Didn't Haruaki Usui scout you for the baseball team? When you were in middle school, you got a reputation for causing trouble at sports tournaments."

"I was scouted? I don't really remember, I guess... Either way, there's no chance in hell I'd play high school baseball. Besides, I'm way too delicate for those brutal practices. The go-home club suits me much better."

He may not be one of the Superhuman Three, but maybe Kamiuchi is pretty incredible, too...

"...Uh, Yuri?"

"Y-yes?"

"Are you by any chance really smart or something?"

"Huh? Oh, I, um... Not at all."

"Yuri always has the top scores in Class 1," the president answers lightly.

Third-year Class 1? That's the class for the elite humanities students aiming for Tokyo University. If she's the head of the pack in there, then...

"Th-that's only because you're in the science class. If you were in humanities, I know you'd be better than I am..."

"Oh, just so you guys know, I got the second-best score on my entrance exam," Kamiuchi chimes in. "Looks like we're both second fiddles who can't hold a candle to those cheaters at the top, Yuri."

"O-oh..."

It seems he's no slouch, either.

"Hmm. I'm beginning to see some commonalities among us. All at the top of our classes... Well, I can't generalize too much, since we're dealing with both sciences and humanities classes here, but it seems we're all the first- and second-best students in our respective years. It's consistent with the number of people."

"Uh, but my grades are only slightly above average. I did pretty good on my finals, but even then, I'm still probably at the bottom of the top scorers, so..." I swallow the rest of my comment.

The student council president, Yuri, and Kamiuchi all eye me suspiciously.

...Why? Did I say something that strange just now?

"Just to confirm, Otonashi and Oomine are both number one in their classes, right?" the president says, looking at me.

I nod silently.

"I see." She has a pleasant look on her face as she speaks, but her eyes are not smiling. *"Then why are you the only one who's different?"*

I flinch in the face of her overpowering question.

What gives? Why are they looking at me like this?

"You can only afford to be so eager."

The president's gaze moves away from me...to Maria.

"Why're you getting so intense before you even know what this game is about? Does that mean you agree with the killing and are all for taking part in it? If so, then you're the one we need to be on guard against."

"Th-that's right. It's not like anything has started yet..."

Prompted by Maria's words, Yuri peeks over at the president as she gives her two cents. In response, the president stands quietly with her lips pursed for a moment. She doesn't seem especially miffed, but more like this is just a habit of hers when she's thinking.

She draws her mouth into a line, then lets out a long breath and replies, "You're right. Maybe it is a bit crazy to start suspecting someone just because they don't fit the theory that all of us are overachievers. Carrying around baseless suspicions could trip us up at some point."

"If you want my input, the most suspicious of us all is our high and mighty president here with her penchant for jumping the gun," Daiya says.

"Ha-ha-ha, I'm suspicious? Go take a look in the mirror."

Daiya smiles happily at the president's words.

"...Uh, what are we doing here? Are we already trying to find the culprit?"

The question shows an obvious inability to keep up with the situation, and the president's mouth quirks upward slightly. "I don't know if I would say we're finding the culprit so much as just figuring out who we need to be on guard against. One of us could be the mastermind orchestrating this game, or maybe the mastermind's accomplice who's trying to facilitate the killing. Basically, if I can learn who they are, then I want to expose them before we pass the point of no return."

The mastermind, eh?

Mastermind or whatever...*I already know who the culprit who set all of this in motion is.*

Daiya Oomine. There is no other possible culprit aside from him.

...But I'm beginning to understand that I can't simply say this.

There isn't any room for clumsy announcements here. I'm already under suspicion simply because my grades aren't high enough. Going against the flow would only make them doubt me even more.

I wonder what would happen if I just said Daiya caused all of this by using the powers of his Box as an owner.

It would sound totally absurd. The only thing that would accomplish would be to convince them I cooked up some crazy lie to get Daiya in trouble.

That's why I can't say anything about the Box, no matter how right I am.

I'm sure the reason Maria is just brooding in silence is because she understands this, too.

"NoW_then_now_then_now_then. I_can_SEe_thaT_the_pARAnoia_is_reALly_StarTing_to_kick_in. I'm_happy_to_seE_thiNGs_are_going_as_expECTed."

We all simultaneously turn our gazes to the big monitor in the center of the wall. On the screen is the same decidedly un-cute bear from before. Seeing it on an even larger screen just makes the creepy factor all the more apparent.

The president sneers at the monitor. "Well, if it isn't the scarebear."

"Watch your mouth and call me Mr. Noitan. Just because you're the student council president of a single school doesn't mean you don't smell like piss, so don't get any ideas you're something special."

The president is smiling confidently, but Yuri lets out a small yelp and shrinks in shock at Noitan's sudden sharp tongue and upsetting sprite.

...She isn't especially short, but there's definitely something about her that reminds me of a small animal... People often say the same about me, though, so it's not like I can talk.

"Just get on with the explanation, scarebear."

"Are you too dumb to understand language? I hope you die first."

"Hey, Your Presidency. We won't get anywhere at this rate, so how about you pipe down for a bit?"

"Fine, fine."

In response to Daiya's caustic remark, she shrugs and closes her mouth. After a bit of silence, the image of Noitan returns to normal, and his speech resumes its normal unsteady manner. He's probably calmed down.

"NoW_I_wiLl_eXPlain_*Kingdom_Royale*."

We watch the screen quietly.

"THis_is_a_gaME_of_KIll_or_be_killED_but_MoRe_precISEly_it_is_a_gAMe_of_sEIzing_the_THRone."

We all look at one another as we listen to Noitan's explanation.

"As_tHE_plAYers_of_this_game_YOu_wiLL_each_be_assIGNed_a_Class. The_Classes_aRE_King_Prince_Double_Sorcerer_Knight_and_Revolutionary. EaCH_has_its_own_aBILIties."

"And how will we know our Class?"

"YoU_can_cHECk_your_Class_oN_the_MONitor_in_your_rOOM. By_the_way_ThEY_are_tOUch_SCREens_so_yOU_can_oPERAte_them_iN_vARIous_ways_dEPENDing_on_your_Class."

The president scowls as she listens to the rest.

"NoW_then_beFORe_I_tell_you_aBOut_the_Classes_I_will_explAIn_the_seTTINg_of_*Kingdom_Royale.* This_kingDOm_is_rULed_by_a_despotIC_KINg_who_has_TRIed_to_inVAde_other_lands_many_times. And…"

"Noitan."

Maria cuts off the bear as he begins to launch into a prologue like the ones people usually skip when they play video games.

"WHAt_is_it_Maria?"

"We don't need all that. Just cut to the chase and tell us what we have to know about the game."

"What the hell sort of attitude is that to take when someone is kindly trying to give you a thorough briefing? You've got a lotta nerve for a kid who reeks of piss."

He's back to the bloodshot eyes.

"You just said Shindo smelled like piss, too. Your vocabulary is weak."

"If a bird trapped in a cage has time to kvetch over that, then you should probably spend it thinking about how to stay alive."

Seemingly satisfied (?) now that he's said his piece, Noitan's image returns to normal.

"LoOKS_like_I_DoN't_have_a_choiCE. I'll_juST_tell_yoU_the_maIN_pOInts. FirST:_The_timETaBLe_must_be_strictLY_OBServed. Break_it_aNd_you_wiLL_be_automATiCally_Eliminated_so_be_cAReFul."

"…What happens to us if we're Eliminated?"

"Compulsory_execution."

The air grows tense.

"By_behEADIng_NAtURally. Idiots_who_CAN't_keep_a_schEDUle_deseRVE_to_die."

Yuri's eyes are wide and unblinking. As she comes to understand that "execution" means exactly that, the color drains from her face.

Noitan continues without a care about her reaction. "THEre_is_also_an_overall_TIMe_limIT. YoU_have_SEVen_pACks_oF_rations. EnOUgh_for_exaCTly_one_week. They_are_maGIC_raTIOns. You_can_eAT_only_one_MEAl_a_DAy_and_not_get_hunGRY. BuT_if_you_don't_eat_at_LEASt_once_a_day_yOU_wilL_STArve_and_be_muMMIfied."

"Mummified... Huh." The president purses her lips while scratching her head. "So how do we win this game? I have no idea what we're supposed to be doing."

"WeLL_the_conditions_for_vicTorY_aRe_diffeRENT_for_each_Class. FoR_exAMPle_the_King_wins_if_he_disPOSes_of_all_those_guNNINg_for_hIS_throne. I'll_sHOw_yOU_the_details_for_eACH_now."

Noitan vanishes, and text appears on the screen.

☆ The King

A king who assassinated his predecessor to seize the throne and has since conducted many invasions. He is extremely suspicious by nature and plots the murder of any and all who would threaten his position of power. The king is unaware that his paranoia has cost him the loyalty of his subjects.

He can ask his servants to commit Murder, but he cannot force them for fear they will turn against him.

There is no bright future in store for the kingdom under the rule of one who cannot trust others such as he.

Abilities of the King

- Murder

  The King selects someone he wants to have killed and can then ask the Sorcerer or the Knight to carry out the act. The King may opt not to choose anyone, too.

- Switch Places

  The King may trade places with the Double for one day only and avoid being the target of Assassination. If the King is targeted during the day while he is switching places, the Double will die instead of the King.

Victory Conditions for the King

Retain hold of the throne (dispose of the Prince and the Revolutionary, who threaten his position).

☆ The Prince

An ambitious man. Originally third in line to succeed for the throne, he took advantage of the suspicious nature of the King to have the other princes assassinated and is now the immediate heir. He is very wary of being suspected and has thus mastered anti-magic techniques.

If he ascends the throne, the kingdom will most likely become even more despotic.

Abilities of the Prince

• Anti-magic

The Prince may not be killed by Magic.

Victory Conditions for the Prince

Become the king (dispose of the King, Double, and Revolutionary).

☆ The Double

A former peasant who both respects the King and closely resembles him. Though he lacks ambitions of his own, he will absolutely never allow the Prince, who has continually mocked him, to seize the throne.

If a man with no aspirations such as he becomes king, the land will fall into ruin in no time at all.

Abilities of the Double

• Succession

If the King dies, or if Switch Places is used, the Double will have the ability to use Murder.

Victory Conditions for the Double

All people trying to kill him die (the Prince and the Revolutionary die).

☆ The Sorcerer

A servant of the King. He is close with the Prince and is also his instructor in all things magical. The Sorcerer is content as long as he is free to conduct his arcane research and has no interest in the throne. No matter how effective his magic proves, no one sees the value of the person holed up in his shell.

Abilities of the Sorcerer

• Magic

The Sorcerer may decide whether to actually kill characters selected for Murder. Characters he does kill become charred corpses.

Victory Conditions for the Sorcerer

Survive.

☆ The Knight

A subordinate of the King. Though in service to the throne, he is actually plotting revenge against the royal family that brought ruin to his homeland. The Knight believes he will only know happiness once the final member of the royal dynasty has been extinguished.

Naturally, one such as he who is consumed by feelings of loss will only fall to the darkness of despair.

Abilities of the Knight

• Death by Sword

The Knight may decide whether to actually kill characters selected for Murder. This ability may only be used if the Sorcerer is dead. Characters he does kill will die by decapitation.

Victory Conditions for the Knight

Achieve vengeance (the King and the Prince die).

☆ The Revolutionary

The right hand of the King. As a capable man, he has come to realize that the kingdom is doomed at this rate and is thus prepared to take up the mantle himself and lead the land.

It will never be possible for a ruler who has earned so much ire through assassinations to successfully guide the kingdom. The only fate that awaits him is to be assassinated himself.

Abilities of the Revolutionary

• Assassinate

The Revolutionary can Assassinate a character he specifies. He may also not choose anyone. The characters he kills will leave a strangled corpse.

Victory Conditions for the Revolutionary

Become the king (kill the King, the Prince, and the Double).

*The game ends when all the victory conditions of those still alive are fulfilled.

Everyone is so absorbed in reading and trying to work through the implications that they don't utter a single word.

I stare at the screen with all my might, too, but that doesn't give me any clue of what I should do next. All I know is that the ominous words "Murder" and "Assassinate" prove that we really will be killing one another in this game of *Kingdom Royale.*

"Hey, scarebear. How exactly do we use these Magic or Assassinate abilities?" the president asks.

"Commands_foR_thoSe_ABIlities_will_aPPear_on_tHE_monitoRs_in_your_rOOms. ALL_yoU_nEEd_to_do_iS_preSS_the_BUTton_TO_perfORm_the_COMMand. YoU_can_KIll_as_easy_aS_you_woULD_bUy_a_train_TICket."

Except for mine, everyone's faces turn white. I look at Maria, unable to understand why they're reacting so strongly.

"...Maria, I—"

"Don't you see how dangerous this situation is?"

I nod slowly. Daiya looks at me with an exasperated smile... I mean, if I don't get it, I don't get it.

"Let's say you feel you're in danger... No, maybe that's not good enough. Let's say you've realized your death is almost certain. The only way to avoid this threat would be to kill a certain person. Would you be able to murder that person with a knife, Kazuki?"

"A-absolutely not."

"How about if all it took was a press of a button?"

"Huh...?"

I could save my life with a single button, in exchange for the life of another.

"......I—I don't think I could do that, either. Kill someone, I mean."

"True, I'm sure you couldn't. But do you think the others would arrive at that same conclusion?"

I instinctively take a look around me.

The student council president, the lady of action. The seemingly cowardly Yuri. The strangely easygoing Kamiuchi. And then Daiya, the owner.

"Do you have any conclusive proof that any of the six of us here, including you, wouldn't take someone else's life the moment they sense danger? ...Let's be honest here. I know I don't."

I'm almost positive that goes for everyone else, too.

"'Someone here could very well kill me.' The thought will probably cross all our minds. I think it goes without saying that paranoia will make the situation especially critical, don't you agree?"

"B-but even if we could kill one another just by pressing a button, it's still not an easy thing to do."

"How about if we're running out of time?"

"...Time?"

"It's like that green bear said. There's an overall time limit—namely, that we die if our rations run out. If there's no victors at that point, then we all lose... We die, in other words."

I swallow.

"Our goal isn't simply to win; it's to find a way out of the game. But if we start running out of time, that goal will start breaking down. Someone will abandon the idea of achieving it at all. This person will probably prioritize survival. They'll even start thinking that if we're all going to die anyway, they may as well fulfill their own conditions for victory. And then once there's a corpse...it's all over."

"...Why?"

"There's a dead body. That means we know someone is actively taking part in the game. If we rest on our laurels, they'll end up killing us all. The rest of us will be forced to play the game as well. And that most likely means there will be no end until a victor is decided."

No one contradicts Maria as she calmly lays out the facts. We're all on the same page, it seems.

"The moment the first body appears, it's all over..."

The bottom line is, we need to think of a way out of this game before someone makes a mistake.

"So_so_sO_Do_you_uNDerStand_the_gaME_nOW? I'lL_show_YOu_the_timeTABle_noW. MAKe_sure_To_follOW_it_anD_get_whERE_YOu're_going_wiTHIn_five_minutES_Of_the_scheDULed_tiME."

The previous screen vanishes, and a timetable appears.

12 PM <A>

- Break time, standby in your quarters.

12 PM – 2 PM <B>

- Assemble in the common area.

2 PM – 6 PM <C>

- Choose a partner for a Private Meeting by 2:40 PM. You may spend thirty minutes in the room of the character you select.
- The King may choose characters to Murder.
- The Sorcerer may perform Magic (or the Knight may perform Death by Sword).
  (Characters targeted by Magic or Death by Sword will die at 5:55 PM.)

6 PM – 8 PM <D>

- Assemble in the common area.

8 PM – 10 PM <E>

- Meal in your own quarters.
  (If you don't have any rations at this point, you will be mummified and die.)
- The Revolutionary may perform Assassinate.
  (Characters targeted by Assassinate will die immediately after being selected.)

10 PM <F>

- Break time, sleep.

"TherE's_no_nEEd_to_taKe_aNy_noTES. The_cLASs_dATa_anD_the_timetABle_are_on_your_poRTABle_DEVices. YouR_DEVices_alSO_keep_lOGs_of_coNVerSations. I_hoPe_they_comE_in_handY."

"Uh, you mean everything we say here will be recorded?"

"Are you implying you've said something you don't want on record?" The president instantly pounces on Kamiuchi's remark.

"No, I haven't said anything like that..."

"Here's what you're thinking: Any careless statement from here on could lead to someone guessing your Class, right? You're ready and willing to play the game, aren't you?"

Kamiuchi laughs ruefully. "Ha-ha, I don't think anyone would want to give anything away in a situation like this."

I can't blame Kamiuchi for being on guard. I don't want to play this game, either, but I can't help but feel an urge to know the others' Classes. Especially the ones who will be hostile to me, as well as the oh-so-dangerous Revolutionary.

That's why I can see us reading those conversation logs.

But that act in itself could be dangerous. I suspect that if I ever become anxious and read back over past remarks as my own fears start to swallow me, I could get hung up on the most trivial of remarks and descend into even further paranoia.

And then, when I can no longer bear the suspicion any longer, I just might press the switch to kill someone...

...That's it. Giving us the ability to review what's been said was a way to get us to take part in the game, no doubt about it.

"AnYWaY_I_wish_you_all_GOOd_luck. DoN'T_let_the_game_end_with_some_bORIng_outCOme_where_YoU_are_all_muMMIfied."

And with that, Noitan disappears from the monitor.

"That damn scarebear...," the president growls.

Now that the grating robotic voice is gone, silence reclaims the room. Everyone is quiet, not even opening their mouths. Perhaps now that we know all of our conversations will be recorded, it's harder to say anything that isn't absolutely necessary.

In the end, the president breaks the silence. "Otonashi."

"What is it?"

"You were pretty casual about saying our goal is to find a way out of this game, but do you actually think that can be done?"

"Of course I do. You don't agree?"

"I... To be honest, I believe it would be extremely difficult. I mean, I can tell that in here, both logic and intuition are abnormal. I had kinda assumed it wasn't just me, that all six of us felt the same way, but am I right?"

Yuri and Kamiuchi nod. I quickly follow suit.

"Do you really think a place as anomalous as this would really provide a viable means of escape? If so, I'd love to see your evidence."

The words sound light, but her tone makes it clear that she isn't going to stand for any questions one way or the other.

Everyone else is also staring at Maria like they're members of a jury.

...She does have proof to back her claims. She knows that no matter how crazy this place is, we can get out if we do something about the Box.

She briefly glances in my direction, but...

"...It will almost certainly be difficult. But that is our only goal. You may not believe there are any breakthroughs to be found, but our only option is to have faith... Am I wrong?"

She's keeping quiet about the Box after all.

"Yeah, you're right."

It appears the president has accepted Maria's unflinching response.

"President. You said you think it's going to be difficult to escape from here—that means you intend to play this game of murder, right?" With a smug look on his face, Daiya cuts in with another sardonic remark.

"Back at it with the carping, huh? You're wrong. After all, I could never kill anyone. Even if we said the murders committed here weren't crimes, and I could kill someone with just a single button—neither of those things would change the fact that I'd tainted my hands by taking a life. I would bear the weight of that sin until I collapsed under it and my life fell apart. I have enough imagination to know that, so it is categorically impossible for me to go through with it."

Daiya clicks his tongue at her perfect response.

"I'm...the same."

"Aw, everyone here knows you could never do a thing like that, Yuri, m'dear. Oh, and neither could I, just so you know."

"If you're going to jump on the bandwagon, try not to make it so obvious. Yuri aside, there's no way I can believe anything you say."

"Wha—? Hey... C'mon, don't say that, President!"

"Well, the one I trust the least is Oomine, though."

The president is paying him back for that smug jab earlier, but he responds with a cynical grin.

And then he goes and says:

"Yeah. I don't mind killing someone if it suits my purposes, after all."

He just made an enemy out of everyone here without even breaking a sweat.

▶Day 1 <C> Kazuki Hoshino's Room

YOUR CLASS IS THE SORCERER.

I notice the message written on the monitor as soon as I return to my room.

Right. Out of the six, the Sorcerer is the only Class that doesn't have any enemies.

"...Whew."

I let out an instinctive sigh of relief.

Our goal is to not even let *Kingdom Royale* get started. All the same, it does my nerves good to know my position has no obvious enemies.

"...Hmm?"

There's text at the bottom of the screen.

NO TARGET HAS BEEN SELECTED FOR MURDER YET.

Murder. The command that lets the King choose someone he wants to have killed.

If the King does pick a target for Murder, then most likely the command for using Magic—for killing someone—will appear on the screen.

I don't want to think about it. Not someone wanting to kill someone else, or me having to press the button.

"......I'm fine, everything's fine," I whisper, trying to encourage myself. The killing won't start so easily. I'm sure none of the others want to start offing one another, either.

At the very least, there's no way anything will happen during the early stages when we still have plenty of time.

"......"

Is that true?

After all, *Daiya is one of the six participants.*

"HeY_hey_hey_Kazuki. It's_tIMe_for_Private_Meetings."

Noitan shows up with the same unnerving suddenness as ever.

I'm used to him by this point, so I look up at the monitor without a hint of surprise. The bear's mouth flaps up and down, still green and still gross.

"ChOOse_who_YoU_wAnt_to_speak_wiTH. You'll_be_aBLe_to_go_to_thEIR_room_for_jUSt_thiRty_minUTes. If_YoU_cHOose_the_saMe_persON_as_soMEONe_else_whoever_cHOSe_firST_will_GO_firST."

Noitan vanishes from the monitor, replaced by the names of the six players, along with our pictures.

"...What happens if the person I choose picks me, too?"

"NoTHINg_happens. YoU_simPLy_get_twICe_as_lONg_to_taLK," Noitan's voice answers.

I ask something else as I look down at the portable device sitting on the table. "...Um, will the devices show the conversations I have during my Private Meetings to anyone besides me and whoever I'm talking to?"

"No. The_onLY_conVERSAtions_that_can_be_viewed_on_a_device_are_thOSE_heaRD_by_the_device's_owNER. EveN_if_yOU_are_in_tHe_saME_room_the_conVERSAtion_wiLL_noT_bE_recoRDed_unless_you_acTUaLly_oVERhear_it. However_wHO_you_sPEAk_with_during_your_Private_Meetings_will_be_noTED_in_the_oTHers'_records_so_be_caREfuL."

Who should I pick...? Well, I guess there's really only one person.

Of course, I press the button for MARIA OTONASHI.

"NoW_tHEn_waIT_a_bit_foR_evERYone_else_to_choOSE."

I wonder who the others are going to pick...?

...It's just a hunch, but I get the feeling Maria won't choose me. I'm sure she's assuming I'll choose her.

That's why she's going to go with...Daiya.

"OkAY. It_sEEMs_eveRYOne_haS_dECIDed. I'll_sHOW_you_who_they_picked."

Noitan vanishes again, and now names appear on the screen.

Iroha Shindo	→	Koudai Kamiuchi	4:20 PM – 4:50 PM
Yuri Yanagi	→	Iroha Shindo	3:40 PM – 4:10 PM
Daiya Oomine	→	Kazuki Hoshino	3:40 PM – 4:10 PM
Kazuki Hoshino	→	Maria Otonashi	3:00 PM – 3:30 PM
Koudai Kamiuchi	→	Yuri Yanagi	3:00 PM – 3:30 PM
Maria Otonashi	→	Daiya Oomine	4:20 PM – 4:50 PM

As I thought, Maria has chosen Daiya.

And Daiya—

"......Ah!"

Daiya has picked...me?

"Why...?"

I can't think of a good reason... With no idea why he's doing all this in the first place, I don't even know where to start.

Fortunately, it seems I won't be seeing him until after I speak with Maria. I'm glad the order isn't reversed. If my Private Meeting with Daiya came first, he would have me in the palm of his hand. With Maria, I can come up with a plan of action.

I take a look at who the others have picked. Yuri's and Kamiuchi's choices are pretty much what I would have expected, but I'm a bit surprised to see that the class president singled out Kamiuchi.

"ThE_dOOr_will_open_onCE_it'S_tIme. Don't_wORry. AFTer_you_pass_through_the_dOOR_you_wiLL_autoMATIcally_go_tO_the_correCT_room."

▶Day 1 <C> Private Meeting with Maria Otonashi – Maria Otonashi's Room

The blackness makes it seem as if I might fall into a void, but when I take a step out into it, I find a room almost identical to my own on the other side. In fact, it's so similar that it feels like the room I left simply rotated around me to become my destination.

"There you are."

Sitting on her bed gazing at me, Maria pats the bed and beckons me to sit next to her.

"We don't have any time for small talk, so let's get right down to business."

"...Um, and what exactly is that?"

"How we're going to get the Box away from Oomine, what else? Don't tell me you actually plan on playing along with this *Kingdom Royale*?"

Sitting next to Maria, I vigorously shake my head no.

"We're going to put an end to the Game of Indolence. Our objective is the same as always. The only thing that's a bit easier this time is that we already know who the owner is."

"...But I wonder if Daiya will hand over the Box..."

Maria's brow furrows a bit at my words. "...That's true. We have to find a way to persuade Oomine..."

"Do you think that'll be difficult?"

"Do you think it'll be easy?"

I shake my head. We can't persuade him. That means we won't be able to get him to produce the Box on his own.

In that case, our only option is to crush it by force. Namely, crush Daiya himself.

"...Hey, Maria. If Daiya loses at *Kingdom Royale*, do you think it would spell the end of the Game of Indolence, too?"

"That all depends on the nature of the Game of Indolence, so I can't really say... But thanks to the Rejecting Classroom, I had plenty of opportunities to learn about Daiya's personality. After observing him for so long, I think *if Daiya has made it so others die if they lose his game, he will die if he loses, too.* I'm sure you agree, right?"

I nod. While I can't be certain as long as I don't know what Daiya's endgame is...it's hard to believe someone as prideful as Daiya would exempt himself from the rules of his game.

"......Hey."

Maria gazes deep into my eyes as I mull over the situation.

"Kazuki... Do you hope Oomine will die?"

"Huh?"

She looks as collected as ever, but I can see the slightest hint of unease in her face as she watches me.

...Of course she would be. It's not too farfetched to think my last question implies we should get rid of Daiya.

"No. I'd never want Daiya to die, I can tell you that."

"...I see," Maria says, and the smile flickering across her face is clearly born from a sense of relief.

...Which makes sense. There's no reason she'd want to resort to such methods.

"Getting out of here because Daiya's dead isn't a real solution," I continue.

"Yeah. You're right."

"Still, that doesn't leave us any closer to figuring out what to do..."

At my noncommittal reply, Maria scowls and starts to speak.

"...I'm a bit reluctant to do this. But I think we may need to enlist the aid of the others aside from Oomine...particularly Shindo. If all of us are on the same page, then we have nothing to fear from *Kingdom Royale*."

"...What do you mean?"

"If we can get them to understand the gist of what Boxes are and convince them that Oomine is the owner, then we can make it clear who everyone's real enemy is. We can avoid the worst-case scenario, where no one knows who's going to kill who. *Kingdom Royale* will never even start as long as no one falls prey to paranoia."

"...But it'll probably be hard to convince them about the Box, huh?"

"Yes, exactly. It's going to be difficult to even bring it up when drawing attention puts you directly in the line of fire."

"Yeah... I can understand why you'd be reluctant to do it."

"...I'm not saying that because I think I'd have trouble pulling it off."

"Huh?"

"Don't you get it? I talk about who the owner is. I inform everyone that their real enemy is Daiya Oomine. *And once I do that, they will all know that Oomine's death will set them free. And they can kill someone with a single button.*"

I automatically choke back what I was going to say.

"Oomine isn't the type to be easily persuaded. Even if Shindo and the others learn the truth, he's unlikely to call off the Game of Indolence. What do you think the others will do when they see that? Do you really think they're all going to wait patiently for him to change his mind when we have a time limit, and when they could be killed as well? I don't think so. If things come to a standstill, it's possible that—"

Maria finishes her sentence with some difficulty.

"—Shindo will kill Oomine."

"That—" I stop and take a big breath before continuing, "That isn't necessarily true... I—I mean the president said herself, right? That she could never kill anybody."

"That was enough to put you at ease?"

"...Do you think she was lying?"

"I don't know whether everything was a lie. However, if Shindo was being sincere, that just makes her all the more dangerous."

"Wh-why...?"

Without a word, Maria stands up, takes the portable device sitting on the table, and fiddles with it. It plays back a voice recording.

"I would bear the weight of that sin until I collapsed under it and my life fell apart. I have enough imagination to know that, so it is categorically impossible for me to go through with it."

"Do you see the danger in these words?"

I shake my head.

"Here's what Shindo is saying: *She can kill as long as she is prepared for her life to fall apart.*"

That sure seems like a really shrewd conclusion, but...yeah, I guess I can see how you might interpret it that way?

"B-but there's no way she would be prepared to ruin her life without an extremely important reason."

"Do you think she wouldn't have one? I can come up with one right now. Let's see... Wouldn't saving Yanagi constitute a really good reason in Shindo's book?"

I fall silent at how easily she fires back. That would definitely give the president enough motivation to cross the line.

That's right—we aren't in the regular world. This is an abnormal place twisted by the Box. *This means many "extremely good reasons" could exist here.*

"Kazuki, I'm sure you know this, but I cannot kill, no matter the reason."

"Yeah, I know."

"I believe you are the same. Can you give an instantaneous explanation, like Shindo did?"

Her words make me wonder.

Why can't I kill anyone?

...Is it because I believe it's arrogant for a person to assume it's okay to kill another?

...Is it because I feel pity when I imagine myself as the victim?

...Is it because my sense of ethics won't allow it?

I can come up with several, but none of them really fit the bill. I don't think they're totally wrong, but they're also not right. They're all reasons you'd apply after the fact, and the resulting inability to kill actually comes first.

"Can't come up with anything, huh?"

"...Yeah." I respond with my head hanging low.

"That's for the best."

"Huh?"

"What Shindo said about her imagination, it isn't right. Those who are truly incapable of killing others don't need any reasons. You and I—*we simply cannot do it.*"

...She's right. That's exactly how it is. It feels more correct to me than anything else.

"Coming up with some pretext for why you can't kill and then expounding on it without a hitch—*that's* unnatural. That speech of Shindo's was nothing more than lip service to a case that she isn't dangerous. But I still think that's more levelheaded than acting blatantly hostile like Oomine."

"Why would Daiya do that when he has to know it would place him in danger…?"

"Well, given his normal attitude, the claims of 'I could never kill anyone' from Shindo and the others probably don't sound very convincing to him. If you think about it, his personality actually places him at a disadvantage in *Kingdom Royale*."

…There's no denying that his general behavior would seem to make him the biggest target.

In contrast, the safest would be Yuri, oddly enough.

"True. There's one thing I'm curious about, though: Is the Game of Indolence an external type or an internal type?"

Maria's gaze sharpens at my question.

"S-sorry, I didn't think before I asked. Y-yeah, a Box as messed up as this would have to be an internal—"

"It's external."

"…Huh?"

"The Game of Indolence is an external-type Box. As for level, I'd say it's around a five."

I'm pretty sure she said the Week in the Mud was an external level four. That means we're dealing with a Box much more powerful than the one that simply caused people to switch places.

But if it's an external type…

"That means he does possess a certain level of firm belief in this situation… In this case, it's possible the owner has mastered the use of the Box."

I swallow hard at her explanation. That means…we're dealing with something pretty serious here, doesn't it?

"That's why persuading him will be difficult. Up to this point, all the owners still possessed a sense of logic when they used their Boxes, at the end of the day. That's why their wishes lacked confidence and had open seams in them. We were able to dig into those weaknesses and get them to reveal their Boxes."

"…But it won't work like that this time."

In all honesty, I had trouble believing Daiya could use a Box so well.

He's a realist, after all. He seems like exactly the type of person who would have trouble with a Box that consummates a wish—a desire for something that would never happen in reality.

"At any rate, we won't be able to escape its effects on the real world. The memories of what we experience here during *Kingdom Royale* will most likely never vanish, and whatever happens will probably carry over into the real world."

"So that means dying in the game means dying for real...?"

"Yeah, it's best to think that... Just to be clear, death has a massive effect, even when we're talking about an internal type instead of an external type. The only reason I'm here unaffected now after losing my life so many times in the Rejecting Classroom is due to the nature of that Box, because it became as if those deaths never happened. If I had perished during the final 27,756th transfer, I would have died in reality, or at least been affected in some way that would leave me functionally dead."

"...I see."

So that's how things stand.

Dying here is the same as dying for real.

"That's why we cannot allow *Kingdom Royale* to start, by any means."

To be perfectly honest, I hadn't really felt that much danger. Describing this as a game makes it all sound so frivolous, and a "death" delivered with a single button—since this Box is divorced from reality, part of me was sort of treating this like events in a game, after all.

But I was wrong.

Even if a single button is all it takes to kill me or for me to kill, there's no resetting those deaths like we would in a game.

"...Anyway, we don't have time. For now, let's think of what you're going to do in your meeting with Oomine."

"Okay."

We may not have a clue as to how to resolve this situation, but we still need to focus first on what we can do.

"Well, my guess is, the first thing Daiya will do is try to figure out my Class. What do you think?"

"You're probably right... By the way, I should warn you: Unless there are some sort of extenuating circumstances, you should never, ever reveal your Class to Oomine or anyone else."

"Gotcha."

I of course understand the danger of that, but…

"But I can tell you, Maria. I'm the Sorcerer."

"…And what would you do if my Class pit me against you?"

"Nothing. I'd still tell you."

"…I see. I suppose that's how it should be. You and I wouldn't hide such a trivial thing from each other."

Maria smiles as she says this, and I feel my face relax a bit at the sight of it.

The information could place our lives in danger if someone else found out about it, and she had just described it as "a trivial thing."

"As it happens, my Class is the Prince. I would've been more relieved if I had gotten the Revolutionary."

I hear that. The one most likely to kill someone is the Revolutionary, the only Class that can dispatch others autonomously. But Maria would never make such a mistake, even if the time limit was approaching.

There is no doubt in my mind that Maria could never kill anybody.

"……Ah."

As the thought crosses my mind, something comes to my attention.

"What is it?"

"U-um…"

Maria looks at me questioningly as I glance at her out of the corner of my eye, and I think:

Maria is powerless within this Box.

I mean, *Kingdom Royale* is a game of murder and deception. Maria can't do either, so she has no chance of winning.

In all our past struggles involving Boxes, I was completely reliant upon her. I'm sure I'll need her help this time around, too.

But—I'm sure a time will come when I'll have to rely on my abilities alone to do what I have to.

"……It's nothing."

Maria frowns and keeps scrutinizing me as I respond.

She has put her faith in my inability to kill someone else. But if I learned of a future where Maria would die, and that I could prevent it by killing someone, then I…

…What would I do?

▶Day 1 <C> Private Meeting with Daiya Oomine – Kazuki Hoshino's Room

As for what I'd need to do to make it through my time with Daiya—the conclusion we eventually reached was complete silence.

Daiya will undoubtedly try to throw me off my game, so even just reacting presents dangers. It's not like I have any faith in my ability to evade his schemes, so all I can do is not listen.

I raise my hand in greeting as Daiya enters my room. After taking a quick glance around the room, he sits on the table.

"Kazu, there's something I want to ask you straight off the bat that—"

"Daiya."

I cut him off immediately.

"I know this is the inside of your Box. All I can think is that you're approaching me because you figure I'm an opponent to deal with and you're hoping to entrap me. So that's all I'm gonna say, and nothing more."

Daiya seems momentarily surprised by my serious, steady delivery, but his expression soon warps with contempt.

"What're you talking about, Kazu?"

"......"

"What do you hope to accomplish by giving me the silent treatment? Aren't you the one who should have questions for me about my Box? I'm sure you have to do something about it."

"......"

I'm not saying a single word. I've made my resolve. If I decide it's okay to just answer one question, Daiya will seize that opening, I'm sure. He'll slowly lure me into believing it's safe to talk to him, then get what he wants out of me. So I'm not giving a peep.

"...I get it—you've left all the decision-making to Otonashi, haven't you? She's the one who suggested you keep your mouth shut, didn't she? You're garbage, Kazu. I've taken shits worth more than you. If all you're gonna do is stay silent, insects still have you beat. At least they'll never talk."

I cover my ears with my hands.

"I know you can still hear me. Hmph, I'll let you in on a little secret, Kazu."

Daiya stands up, leans in toward my ear, and whispers:

"This Box is not the result of my wish."

My eyes widen of their own accord at his words, and I look up at him.

Daiya cackles so hard I almost wonder if he's gone crazy.

"See? Less than a bug."

"Ngh..."

Why am I letting him get to me?! It's impossible for me to stay quiet in the face of this!

After his laughter subsides, Daiya returns to the table. He then regards me for a moment and speaks again.

"But what I just told you is the truth."

...He won't fool me. There's no way I'll believe him. I'm not that much of a sucker.

"Anyway, I know it's no use telling you to trust me. No matter how empty your head is, you aren't just gonna swallow everything I say hook, line, and sinker. But let me ask you: Why do you think I would make a point of saying what I did?"

Daiya smiles as he continues:

"Because it's the truth."

...I don't believe you. I cannot, will not believe you.

"I'm sure you know. I didn't do anything for a while after I obtained a Box. In short, *I had a Box in my possession, but I didn't use it*. Come on, Kazu. *Can you really say that isn't still the case?*"

I swallow hard.

"O grew impatient when I didn't use my Box for a while, so they gave another one to someone else, and that's how we ended up here. Can you really rule out the possibility? How about it, Kazu?"

...It's not possible... I'm sure it isn't.

"I won't ask you to believe me. I'm sure it's impossible for you in the first place. But, Kazu, you must be wondering, aren't you? What I'm telling you could be a lie, but maybe, just maybe, it's the truth. If so, *regardless of whether it's true, you still have to consider the possibility of another owner out there, don't you?* ...Heh, guess that's not for me to say, though."

...Dammit. Daiya's right.

It's not even a dilemma for me. The truth is, I did find it strange that Daiya would be able to use a Box so well. His not being the owner would explain this.

If there is another owner aside from Daiya, it'll be easy to slip up and get myself killed.

And that's how I fall right into Daiya's trap.

He isn't the type to miss his chance now that I'm off-balance and my mental defenses have left an opening.

"Kazu, you're the Sorcerer, aren't you?"

"......What?"

The word slips out of my mouth.

"H-how did you...?"

How did he know? I know I didn't do anything that would've given me awa—

And then the thought led me to a realization.

I did give it away—*just now.*

My face must look really stupid, because Daiya starts cackling delightedly again.

"Ha-ha-ha! I knew you were an idiot, but this game really is way over your head!"

I bite down on my lip as I listen to him laugh away.

Despite all the advice from Maria, in the end it went to waste. Daiya has me completely in the palm of his hand.

"...You've got good luck, Daiya."

Daiya was just guessing when he said the Sorcerer. He had a one-in-six—no, he knows his own Class, so it's a one-in-five—chance of getting it right. It was just coincidence that the one he chose to trick me happened to be my real Class. If I were another Class, he would've only figured out I'm not the Sorcerer, and that would be that...

"Lucky? You don't understand why I decided to ask if you're the Sorcerer, do you?"

"...What do you mean?"

Daiya scratches his head in silence for a moment.

"Hey, so let's say I'm not the owner of this Box."

"That's not what I think."

"Just shut up and listen. If I'm not, then that means I don't want to be a part of this killing game, either. And if that's the case, then the death of a friend like you wouldn't be my real intention."

"...Okay."

"That's why I would want to ask if your Class was the Sorcerer."

"...I don't follow."

After I say this, Daiya regards me with disdain.

"You probably think the Sorcerer is the safest because he doesn't have any enemies, don't you? If you believe that, then it isn't brains you've got in your head but just a big glob of shit."

My words catch in my throat as he hits it right on the mark.

"Let me put this in easy terms even a monkey could understand: The Class with the least chance of survival is without a doubt the Sorcerer."

"...Why? Whether the Sorcerer lives or dies has nothing to do with the victory conditions of the other Classes."

"Even you must know the most dangerous Class is the Revolutionary, right?"

I nod. With the ability to kill autonomously, it goes without saying that the Revolutionary is the most dangerous Class.

"The one the Revolutionary wants out of the way the most is the Sorcerer. You get it, right? The only other Class that can actually choose whether to kill someone is the Knight. The victory conditions of the Knight and the Revolutionary are comparatively similar, which makes it easy for them to plot together. With the Sorcerer out of the picture, the risk of the Revolutionary getting offed drops considerably."

I pick up the portable device on the table and read back over the portion about the Classes.

...He's right. Even if the Revolutionary does away with the King, the Class that seems like his most immediate enemy, he still has the Double and the Prince to deal with, so his situation doesn't really change. But if he gets rid of the Sorcerer, the Revolutionary immediately puts himself at an advantage.

"Wait, so...if the Sorcerer dies, doesn't that make it almost certain that the Revolutionary will win...?"

"It's not that simple. People could still guess the wrong Class for one another, and others most likely aren't going to ally with the Revolutionary so easily. And then—"

Daiya rummages around in my hemp bag, then pulls out that big knife.

"No matter how much of a disadvantage someone is at in the game, they still have this if worse comes to worst. Heh, survival is a cinch in *Kingdom Royale* if you're prepared to kill someone else directly."

My breath catches in my throat.

...I'm certain of it. The owner of the Game of Indolence...is insane.

"...Kazu, lemme tell you something."

Daiya puts the knife away as he speaks.

"You're not going to be able to persuade the owner before the killing starts. If you want to keep the damage to a minimum, then your only chance is to take out the owner. That's why—"

Daiya looks at me. His expression is sincere, without the slightest hint of deception, as he makes his assertion.

"—no matter how much you fight it, it's already set in stone. Someone's gonna die because of this Box."

I give a slight shake of my head, then whisper:

"That's not true..."

Daiya doesn't say anything.

The truth is that even I'm already aware.

I already know that this is the simple truth.

▶Day 1 <D> The Common Area

No one else is there yet when I arrive in the common area.

I think back over my meeting with Daiya. In the end, I spilled the beans that I'm the Sorcerer, as he hoped, and now I'm not even certain he's the owner.

In light of all that, I need to discuss what to do next with Maria. I rushed to the common area because I wanted to speak with her as soon as possible—and just as I think this, she steps through the door.

"Maria!"

I call out to her, and she gives me a stern look as she seats herself in the chair across from mine.

Maria should have had a Private Meeting with Daiya after ours ended. From the look on her face, I'm guessing he got to her just like he did with me.

"...Did something happen with Daiya?"

"......I think it might be similar to what happened with you. I've been basing my approach on the assumption that Daiya is the owner, but now I've come to consider the small chance it could be someone else. If so, it's going to be more difficult than ever to talk to the others about Boxes."

"And we don't have time, either..."

"Yeah, that's what is troubling me. I would like to use this time to chit-chat with the others to get a grasp on each of their personalities, but small talk has never been my forte. Probably because it's pretty much impossible to talk about my own past without mentioning Boxes."

Maria's past, huh?

I know pretty much nothing of her personal history, myself. Maria doesn't speak about herself without prompting, and knowing about the Misbegotten Happiness as I do, I just can't bring myself to ask.

"Maria, um—"

"Yo."

Kamiuchi turns toward us and waves as he arrives in the common area. I smile awkwardly and return the gesture.

I curl my hand into a C shape and put it up to Maria's ear so Kamiuchi won't overhear what I say.

"Kazuki, whispering won't work. If we show the others that we're trying to hide what we're doing, it'll just make them wary of us."

"Oh, I see..."

"Maricchi, you don't gotta worry so much. Coupla lovebirds like you are bound to have one or two secrets."

"You say that, but that doesn't necessarily apply to the others."

"Guess you're right. Everybody's so scary anyway. Especially the president and Daiya."

"...Maria, do you know Kamiuchi from before?"

I ask this because of how familiarly they're speaking to each other.

"No, not at all."

"Whoa, kinda harsh, don't you think? We've talked a few times before, you know."

"You've tried to talk to me several times in the past, but we've never had a conversation."

Kamiuchi shrugs with an exasperated look. "All I'm trying to do is soothe my troubled soul a bit by speaking with a girl too beautiful for this world. No need to get all defensive. It's not like I'm plotting to pry you off Hoshino there."

"...Listen, Kamiuchi. Just so you know, Maria and I aren't seeing each other, got it?"

"C'mon now, it's a little late to be modest or humble or whatever."

Seems there's no point in telling him otherwise.

As we're talking, the rest of the players arrive in the common room. At the president's direction, we all take our seats.

"Now then, has anyone thought of a way to escape *Kingdom Royale*?"

With that opening question, the president smiles and crosses her arms as she waits for someone to speak up. I steal a glance at Daiya and see that he's not even facing us, as if he's paying no attention at all to the discussion.

If the three of us who are in the know about Boxes can't say anything, then most likely no one will have anything to offer. —At least, that's what I thought, but then to our surprise, someone timidly raises their hand.

"Oh, Yuri. You got something?"

"Um, it's not a way to escape so much as a way to stop the game... Is that okay?"

"Oh, awesome! Go ahead and tell us your idea!"

At the president's prompting, Yuri gives a tiny nod.

"Well...if I'm not wrong in assuming...we all agree that paranoia will make our situation worse, right?" Once we've all nodded our assent, Yuri continues, "We don't know who is what Class. We don't know who is whose enemy in the game. I believe that's why everyone is so uneasy. None of us wants to proceed with the game, right? If that's the case, then wouldn't it be better for us all to just come out and tell one another our Classes?"

Everyone is more than a little shocked by this timidly delivered yet very bold proposal.

Though Yuri seems a bit taken aback by our reaction at first, she musters her courage again and says, "If we do that, no one will be able to get the jump on anyone else anymore. I think we'll all be able to trust one another. If we all do it at once, then no one will be able to lie. We'll know someone isn't telling the truth if more than one person says the same Class. So...how about it?"

"Oh man, Yuri, you're amazing! That's absolutely perfect!"

Yuri smiles shyly and blushes at Kamiuchi's enthusiastic agreement.

"We can only do this while all six of us are together in one place. If even one of us is missing, then it will be possible for someone to lie... Oh, someone being missing is pretty bad, isn't it? I'm sorry I mentioned it."

Yeah, that's a good idea…I think. But I can't agree to it that easily. We might be overlooking something.

Maria is probably in the same place. After spending a moment in thought with her arms folded, she says:

"I agree."

She didn't find anything wrong with it when she thought it over? If not, then I've got no problem with it.

But just as I've made up my mind to let everyone know I'm all in…

"Hmph." Daiya snorts in derision.

A mixture of bewilderment and fear appears on Yuri's face in response.

"…You don't like the idea, Oomine?"

"I don't."

"I'm sorry if I didn't think things through enough… Would you explain why you disagree, if you don't mind?"

"I don't like how you're pretending to be a Goody Two-shoes."

Yuri's eyes go wide, and she freezes at this unexpected reply.

"What's with that face? Can you only comprehend language when it's what you wanna hear? I'm saying I'm not going along with your idea because I hate *you*, you piece of shit."

Tears begin to well up in Yuri's eyes.

"Oomine. Come on, don't you think that's a bit much? Please apologize to Yuri here."

"What? Me, apologize? The rest of you should be thanking me. I'm the one whose exposing her for trying to play dirty. Isn't that right, Yanagi?"

Yuri's shoulders jump in surprise as the tears threaten to fall.

"I-I'm p-playing dirty? Why…?"

"Well, then let me ask you this: Are you the Revolutionary or the Sorcerer?"

Yuri's face instantly goes white.

"You're not either, right?"

"…H-how did you know…?"

"The truth is that you've figured it out. You know that the risk each Class faces by revealing itself is completely different. Which means you aren't one of the two Classes that are the biggest targets. You're one of the relatively safe ones, right?"

Yuri's already pale face continues to blanch, and I'm starting to feel bad for her.

"Disingenuous as you are, you suggested this plan because it helps you, not because it makes our situation any better, didn't you?"

At Daiya's hostile tirade, the tears finally spill from Yuri's eyes.

"Oh, come on, do you really think I'll let your little scam slide if you cry? Man, a woman's tears really are a handy trick. I'm sure a slut like you can probably turn it on and off like a faucet, eh?"

"That's horrible... How can you say that...?"

"All you want to do is find out who the dangerous Classes are so that you can keep yourself alive."

"That's...not... I just hate the idea of us killing one another, that's all..."

Yuri lowers her face, unable to stop the flow of tears running down it.

...It's true. If someone as seemingly cowardly as Yuri were the Revolutionary or Sorcerer, she most likely wouldn't have proposed such a dangerous idea.

But despite this, she gave it her all to come up with a plan that could improve our situation. Daiya was way out of line to say what he did. Apparently of a similar opinion, Kamiuchi gives Daiya a look like he's about to start swinging any second.

"You probably just didn't want to have to say anything because you're the Revolutionary, aren't you? Sorry, but if you're the Revolutionary, I really don't feel like letting you run the show here."

"Oh, so I'm the Revolutionary, am I? If so, then I'll just have to Assassinate you during this next <E> period."

Daiya's reply is even more hostile than Kamiuchi's, and the younger boy is totally speechless, probably overwhelmed. Apparently losing his desire to fight back, Kamiuchi frowns and stays silent.

"Anyway, even if I wasn't against it, this plan would never work. Isn't that right, President?"

Yuri raises her tear-soaked face and looks at the president, who returns her gaze with a rueful smile and then speaks.

"...Yeah, that's true. Sorry, Yuri. I'm against the idea, too."

"Wh-why...?"

"The idea definitely has some merit, as you mentioned. It's just that the disadvantages are too big. For example, if that scumbag Oomine really was the Revolutionary, do you think the rest of us would be able to stay calm? If things went poorly, we might even end up more paranoid that before."

"But that's…"

"That would probably prompt Oomine to act, too. He might even flaunt his power and try to control the rest of us. I can think of plenty of ways things could get worse. That's why I'm fundamentally against the idea."

"……I see."

Now that even her friend the president has rejected the idea, Yuri's face grows even grimmer.

"Someone as stupid as I am should have just stayed quiet… I'm sorry for any confusion."

Another tear wells up and falls from Yuri's eye.

"Th-that's not true, Yuri. I think it's a really good plan. And see, even Maria agreed to it, too!"

"…Hoshino."

Though my efforts to cheer her up seem a bit forced, Yuri manages to give me a little smile.

"Why *did* you agree with this idea, Maria?" the president asks.

"Because I think reaching a mutual understanding between all of us is more important than anything right now. No one will be able to disclose everything they feel if we don't reveal our Classes or something similar, right? I think if we can do that, things will never reach the point where we start killing one another, but how about you?"

"Isn't that just because you don't feel fear that easily? Not everyone here is as strong as you. To be honest, I've been terrified this entire time."

"You don't seem like it."

"The only reason is because I'm trying to hide it. Showing any weakness in this situation means someone might take advantage of it… Well, telling you about it kinda defeats the purpose, but I'm saying it anyway."

She sounds completely at ease saying this… Yeah, she definitely isn't telling the truth about being scared.

"But it's not wrong to say we need to share our Classes if we want to reach a mutual understanding. The situation is still much too opaque now, though, so I can't help but feel it's too early for that."

"But if someone dies, it'll be too late."

"True. So we need to make a decision soon…," Maria quietly says and pouts her lips. That's her habit when she's thinking. "Well, let's set that aside for today. I'd be surprised if we ended up with a victim today, at least."

★ ★ ★

We didn't come up with any ideas better than Yuri's after that.

Though we discussed all kinds of things in an attempt to build communication among us, we were unable to find what we needed to make any progress before the period ended.

"TiME's_up. Go_bACk_or_you'll_DIe."

Noitan's announcement prompts me to look at my watch, at which point I see that it's eight on the money. The time for <D> is over.

Daiya heads to his room straightaway, while the president and Kamiuchi have just gone through the door themselves.

Welp, guess I'd better head back soon, too, I think, and I'm just about to leave when someone grabs the sleeve of my uniform.

"What is it, Maria?"

I turn around.

It isn't Maria who I find, but a wide-eyed Yuri. As I realize my mistake, my face automatically turns red. Yuri crinkles her eyes in a gentle smile when she sees it.

"U-um...what's up, Yuri?"

"Mm. I just wanted to say thank you."

"...? Thank me?"

As I tilt my head in confusion, for some reason Yuri seems even happier than before.

"If you don't know right away...that means you weren't being nice to me on purpose just so you could get me on your side, then..."

"...Huh?"

"Oh, it's nothing... Do you really not know what I'm talking about? Come on, you tried to cheer me up when I was crying, didn't you?"

"...Oh... So that's what you mean."

"Thanks again."

Seeing Yuri bow deeply toward me, I hurriedly make a reply.

"C-cut it out... It's not like I did anything special."

"But what you did really saved me."

"W-well, in that case...I'm glad..."

All these thank-yous are really making me blush.

For some reason, Yuri's eyes soften into another warm smile as she watches my red-faced antics.

"...I feel like I can trust you, even in a game like this."

"Huh?"

She seems to hesitate for a moment, but as if making up her mind, she looks directly at me and says, "If we can all trust one another, then no one will kill anyone else. I'm sure of it… Hoshino, do you think I'm naive?"

When I return that imploring gaze, I shake my head as hard as I can.

"Not at all. I agree with you."

"Really?"

Seemingly without thinking, she joyfully grabs my right hand in both of hers. Her grip is warm and soft, which makes my face flush all the more.

"If we hold hands like this—and all the others do, too—if we can trust one another like this, there's no way we can lose to this game. So can you and I start it by trusting each other?"

"O-okay…"

I find it hard to look directly into such an untroubled smile, so I can't help but lower my gaze.

Yuri may be an upperclassman…but, man, is she cute.

"Kazuki."

Someone calls my name, and I look up to see Maria watching us with a blank expression… I only figured this out recently, but that's the face she often makes when she's upset.

"We're running low on time. You'd better get back quickly."

"Oh yeah…"

I look at Yuri, and she lets go of my hand, reading my intent. Her expression is somewhat sad, or maybe lonely.

"Yanagi, you should pay attention to the time, too."

"O-okay…"

Yuri still finds Maria frightening, it seems.

"…Hey, Yuri. You can trust Maria; don't worry."

"Oh, yes. If you say so…"

"Well, we'd better all get back to our rooms."

"Yes, you're right… Oh, one more thing."

Yuri brings her lips close to my ear.

"I'll come by for a Private Meeting tomorrow."

She whispers to me, and I can feel her breath on my ear.

As Yuri almost dances away from me, a slightly impish smile appears on her face before she trots off through the door and disappears.

Still in a daze, I stare at the place where she vanished.

"...Hmph."

Maria snorts unhappily, then follows her through the door.

Now alone in the common room, I ruminate over her name.

Yuri Yanagi.

Yanagi.

"...They are...kind of similar."

I don't think their faces have all that much in common. But that mischievous grin she flashed at me before she went through the door does remind me of her.

The other "Yanagi" I know.

I doubt I'll ever see her again, though.

▶Day 1 <E> Kazuki Hoshino's Room

YURI YANAGI WAS STRANGLED TO DEATH BY ASSASSINATE.

This is the message on the monitor in my room.

Unable to process the words, I don't react at all. I just stand there silently, reading it over and over.

She died?

Yuri...died...?

"...What the hell is this?" I mutter without thinking, giving a small laugh.

I mean, everybody said it, right?

There's no way anyone would die on the first day. It's all gonna be okay. That's what they said.

Yeah, I know they did. Hey...that's what's you said, right?!

"HeY_hey_hey."

The incomprehensible text vanishes from the screen as the green bear appears.

"PoOr_Yuri_hAS_dieD."

"Don't lie!!" I find myself yelling at Noitan.

"A_lie?"

Suddenly…

…Noitan's sprite changes to something I've never seen before. His mouth spreads wide enough to tear its face, and it raises itself open.

"Oo-hya-hya-hya-hya-hya-hya-hya-hya-hya_A_lie?_Wouldn't that be nice_ But she's dead_She was strangled_so her eyeballs popped out_and her face turned all purple_and her bowels emptied_and she died_She used to be so cute_and now she's ugly and stinky and dead."

I had thought he was just a creepy bear.

But this is the first time I've ever felt such utter loathing from the depths of my heart.

It's possible this is the true nature of Noitan—no, the Box. This is the truth of this hateful, irredeemable, senseless wish.

"It's really too sad_You two were becoming such good friends_Maybe you coulda hooked up if you played your cards right_But now she's dead_ Too bad_so sad!_Oo-hya-hya-hya-hya-hya-hya-hya-hya-hya-hya-hya-hya-hya-hya-hya-hya-hya-hya-hya!"

The laughter is so grating that I cover my ears.

There's no way I can allow a wish like this to continue. It doesn't matter what kind of troubles led the owner to make a wish like this. I don't care if there are any weaknesses to work on or not. No matter why it came into being, I cannot allow a wish like this to exist.

"Oo-hya-hya-hya-hya-hya-hya-hya-hya-hya-hya-hya-hya-hya-hya-hya-hya-hya-hya-hya!"

That's why this bear is my enemy.

"……Prove it."

"Hmm?"

Noitan's mouth returns to normal.

"Show me some proof that Yuri is dead. If you don't, I'll never believe you."

"Proof_eH?"

"Yeah, I know you're lying, so prove—"

"Fine."

Noitan disappears. At the same time, the door to my room opens.

"…What the hell…?"

The same darkness as before unfolds beyond the door.

I swallow hard as I stand before the black depths. Only now do I pause to think. If everything is as Noitan says it is, then beyond it lies the "proof"...

Regardless, I have no choice but to go through that door—through that darkness.

I plunge through the entryway.

And then, in the center of that backward cell-like room—*there it is.*

"Ah!"

Yuri Yanagi's—xxxxxx.

"A-ahh!"

Irrefutable proof.

I know now. I know it's real.

I comprehend why it's there, but even then, I still can't seem to make the connection. I can't connect this sight to the same girl who was once so pretty.

Despite this, even if I can't associate her with what has become of her, the horrible state of the body alone is enough to break my heart.

I yell, then lose control of myself and collapse. It brings me closer to the xxxxxx. In place of the lovely features one might expect, what reveals itself before my eyes is...

"...U-urgh."

...a visage, purple and monstrous, that threatens to drive even my own pity for her from my mind.

Now I get it; there weren't any falsehoods or exaggerations in Noitan's description. *She's really here, in exactly the state Noitan said she would be.*

Now, I can finally acknowledge the truth.

Yuri Yanagi is dead.

Yet again, I was unable to save Yanagi.

And thus, *Kingdom Royale* begins...

...with the death of the girl who said we would be fine as long as we took one another's hands.

•Yuri Yanagi, dead via Assassinate

▶Day 2 <B> The Common Area

A hemp sack is lying on the table like it's on display.

Its contents are pretty much identical to the one in my room. The only difference is that the digital watch is beige instead of light blue. Yuri's portable device is inoperable.

There are also six sets of rations. This means that if someone dies, we can take their food and extend the time limit. This, too, is most likely a system to encourage murder.

It makes me sick.

All of us sit in our chairs, simply gazing at the sack in silence.

Next to me, Daiya wipes away some blood dribbling from his mouth. Kamiuchi punched him almost as soon as <B> period had started. Kamiuchi believes beyond all doubt that the Revolutionary—the one who killed Yuri—is Daiya.

The president, who had joined Maria in stopping Kamiuchi's outburst, whispers to Daiya: "...Just be happy he didn't use a knife."

At this point, anyone could kill anyone, and it wouldn't come as a surprise.

"You two need to cool off and think things through. Let's confirm something first. The Revolutionary killed Yuri. They killed a kind girl. And the culprit is one of us. There's no mistaking that."

At first glance, the president seems as levelheaded as she did yesterday, but her expression seems, almost deliberately, a little less confident.

Her gaze is also almost unnaturally steely.

"Our goal is to find a way out of *Kingdom Royale*. But now we have a second goal. Namely, *to find the Revolutionary and kill them*. That's fine and well, too."

"Hold on, Shindo. Where do you get off deciding this?"

"Otonashi, I'm sorry, but I'm not going to accept any debate on this. Would you like me to explain? First of all, at this rate, the Revolutionary is going to kill the rest of us, too. Second, if they murdered someone at this point in the game, it's plausible they're the mastermind, or at least an ally of whoever is behind this. Third, I can't stand the thought of them walking all over us."

"You yourself said that killing someone would ruin your life. Does all this mean you're prepared to let your life fall apart now?" Maria asks.

For just a moment, the president struggles to respond. However, her answer is smooth.

"I don't know. But I do know I could never forgive someone for murdering Yuri like that."

"……I see."

I'm guessing Maria has determined that trying to persuade her right now would be pointless, not to mention unnatural. She holds her tongue.

"Our goals are settled. Does anyone have anything else?"

The president surveys us as we sit there with our heads bowed, then starts up again.

"No? Well then, this is just my opinion, but—"

She stops before she can finish and widens her eyes in surprise.

Daiya, who chose not to participate properly in our talks yesterday, has his hand raised.

"Is there something you would like to say?"

"Yeah… Well, I'll stay quiet if you aren't interested in hearing any testimony from the suspect."

"I didn't say that… But why are you speaking up now after staying silent for so long?"

"If this keeps up, I'm almost certainly next, so you can't expect me to keep my mouth shut."

"You have a point."

Kamiuchi snorts at their exchange. "You can say whatever you want. Nothing is gonna change the truth as I see it, so your comments are nothing more than a bunch of white noise to me, got it?"

"Suit yourself." Dismissing him, Daiya turns his gaze on the president. "My question is, why did the Revolutionary decide to target Yuri Yanagi?"

"I'd like to find the answer to that as well," the president says with a small frown on her face, and Kamiuchi lashes out:

"What're you saying? Does any of that matter? What else do we need to know? The Revolutionary is a low-down piece of crap who needs to die!"

"…Kamiuchi, if you were the Revolutionary, and you had to kill someone, would you kill Yanagi first?"

"Would the trash heap please mind not speaking to me before it gets tossed in the incinerator? I'm only sittin' here calmly right now because I know you're going to get wasted by Magic soon enough."

"Ugh… And here I thought he understood how to speak like a human."

Daiya shrugs exaggeratedly.

"What do you think, President? Do you think Yanagi should have been killed first?"

"…Probably not, if it was just for survival. If it did happen to be me, the first person I'd want eliminated is you, Oomine. It's plausible some of the others might want me or Otonashi out of the picture, but I can't imagine anyone getting rid of Yuri right off the bat."

"Right? I suppose it's not unthinkable, if someone learned she was the Sorcerer, for instance, but I figured out that wasn't the case yesterday, so we can scratch that idea."

The president seems slightly irritated as she asks, "I understand what you're saying, but what's your point?"

"Basically, the goal of the Revolutionary was to put us all into this exact situation."

I don't see what he's getting at. But I have the feeling everyone else does. Silence takes hold of the room instantly.

"…Ha-ha." Kamiuchi's sardonic chuckle breaks the silence. "I have no idea what you're going on about. Do we really need to keep beating around the bush? If someone wanted you dead, all they'd need to do is take you out with Assassinate lickety-split, right? The fact that the Revolutionary didn't do that just proves it's you, don't you think?"

"But if I die, then they could get suspected of being the Revolutionary."

Kamiuchi's eyes go wide as he finds himself at a loss for words. As he falls silent, the president speaks in his place.

"*The Revolutionary set you up as a scapegoat*—that's what you're trying to say, isn't it? So why wouldn't that be some lie you came up with to try to get out of this situation?"

"If I were the Revolutionary, I'd have no reason to start with Yanagi."

"Well, that applies to everyone else here, too, don't you think?"

"Not necessarily."

Daiya pulls his portable device from his pocket and presses the playback button.

"*—If that's the case, then wouldn't it be better for us all to just come out and tell one another our Classes?*"

"Yanagi wanted us to be open about our Classes. More than anything, she hoped to keep us from being consumed by fear. That being the case, *there's a good chance Yuri Yanagi had already revealed her Class to someone she could trust.*"

The president and Kamiuchi both fall silent.

"So what do you think? *The two of you had a Private Meeting with Yuri Yanagi yesterday, right?*"

I suddenly remember she tried to set up a Private Meeting with me as well.

If we'd had that meeting today, she most likely would have shared her Class with me.

But—that's right.

She would trust the president more than someone she just met, like me. If so, would she really tell me her Class before she told her?

"...So let's say we did know Yuri's Class. That still doesn't give us a reason to kill her straightaway."

"And that's because our great and wise student council president can't figure it out? ...Heh-heh-heh, then let me fill you in. The reason would be to steal her Class."

...There wasn't anything in *Kingdom Royale* rules about being able to do that.

Still uncertain what he's getting at, I listen to what Daiya has to say.

"They want to convince everyone else I'm the Revolutionary. As the real Revolutionary, they must of course pretend to be another Class. If they said they were Yanagi's Class, then their chances of being found out by the other players would decrease dramatically. The dead tell no tales. If they did ever find themselves having to reveal their Class, they could simply say Yanagi's."

All of us are quiet, waiting for Daiya to continue.

I don't get it, though. Is that really enough to warrant killing her first?

"How about we run a simulation? Let's start by utilizing the advantage of being able to say we're Yanagi's Class since she's already gone, and then suggest that everyone reveal their Class. The victory conditions for the Revolutionary are to kill three people: the King, the Prince, and the Double... Hmm, I would guess that maybe Yanagi was the Prince or the Double."

"...How are you able to narrow it down so much?" Kamiuchi asks with a sullen look.

"If the King gets killed, then the Double will know that someone offed the King. Namely, because they will then be able to use the Murder command. So the Double will lose the ability to deceive others about being the King."

"But there's still the Knight."

"If Yanagi was the Knight, it would be better to find a way to use her than to kill her. I don't need to explain about the Revolutionary or the Sorcerer, right?"

"......"

"Now that the Revolutionary has killed Yanagi, they only need to do away with two other people to win. With pretty much everyone thinking I'm the Revolutionary, there's almost no chance anyone will go after them. If they can successfully ask everyone's Class, they'll be able to identify who they need to kill. I could explain in further detail...but it's too much of a pain, so I'll stop there."

A small smile rises on Daiya's face as he carries on.

"But I'm sure you all know this, right? Setting me up as the Revolutionary will turn the game in their favor, and victory will be all but certain."

And with that, Daiya...

...fixes Iroha Shindo with a glare.

"I'm sure they thought they were pretty badass up until now. To them, everyone else is dim-witted scum that serves no other purpose but making them look better in comparison. They're probably more than happy to kill worthless slugs like that if it helps them survive... And they've got a lot of nerve."

Daiya snorts scornfully, then spits:

"They're just a fool, but they still made an enemy of me."

"......"

A thought suddenly strikes me.

I notice it because I'm still in shock over Yuri's death, which has kept me from speaking and joining the discussion.

What is this?

Right here, right now, we're all snapping at one another. We're hurling hate and accusations, ready to explode at any moment. It's just like the way we imagined *Kingdom Royale* would start, isn't it?

This is bad. We're done for at this rate. I mean, everything is going exactly the way they want it… Exactly the way the owner of the Game of Indolence wants it!

If this keeps up, we're all going to kill one another, and that will be that.

That's the one thing we have to avoid. We must find out exactly who the owner is. We have to work together… We have to, but…

"That's enough out of you, Oomine."

The president's voice is utterly unlike before.

All the anger and loathing she can no longer keep bottled in has contorted her face.

"You've got a lot of gall, throwing out such baseless delusions so confidently. You can sneer from your high horse all you want, but I have no idea where you get off thinking it's okay it to act this way. Otonashi has better grades than you in school, Kamiuchi has you beat physically, Hoshino is more popular than you, and Yuri was more charming. Oh, look, guess you're not the best at anything, huh? If you are, it's your talent for twisting logic."

The president smiles the same sort of condescending smile I would expect from Daiya.

"You're no different from all the other scumbags who can't face reality. No… You're even worse because you actually murdered someone."

At those words, Daiya returns the president's smile with a similar one. The president isn't even pretending to be pleasant anymore.

"We aren't in a nice, soft little world where everyone will leave you alone if you throw your weight around, not anymore. You've made a painful blunder, and you can't write off a mistake like this as youthful indiscretion. You killed Yuri… Haven't you noticed? You're done. Crushing someone as innocent and incompetent and helpless and ineffectual as you will be as easy as stepping on an ant."

She continues on in an unfittingly gentle voice:

"I already recognize you as an enemy, get it? I'm going to do everything in my power to ruin you. Why, I might even—*kill you.*"

"So what?"

"…That's right—you probably need me to spell it out for you, huh? I'll start off by exposing your delusions for what they are. You said Yuri was the Double or the Prince, but that's wrong. You made a simple oversight. The King will know if the Double dies because they will no longer be able to use their Switch Places command. Oh no, what a stupid mistake! That's why if someone was going to kill Yuri to try to say they were her Class, the only thing she could possibly be is the Prince."

Hearing this, I look over at Maria, the real Prince. She continues to watch the two of them go at it with a keen gaze.

"I've got a confession to make. I knew Yuri's Class. Isn't that great, Oomine? At least one little theory of yours was right. But see, she wasn't the Prince. That means one of us here must be. Hey, Your Highness, whoever you are, do you understand that Oomine's full of it now?"

Daiya simply remains quiet, perhaps unable to come up with a good argument.

"You would have noticed all this if you were the King or the Double, so I know you aren't either of those Classes. So what does that leave us with?"

The only ones left are the Knight and the Revolutionary. That's how much the president has narrowed down Daiya's possible Class.

Even then, Daiya only breaks his silence to laugh mockingly at the president.

"Do you really want to take me down that badly? You're really at the end of your rope."

"What?"

"You sure are proud of yourself just for finding a loose thread in my theory. I'm not really the Revolutionary, so naturally, all I can do is make conjectures. All you've accomplished with your blabbering just now is prove your own treacherous nature to all of us. I'll come up with as many new theories as you want. Then you can have fun wasting your time breaking them down."

"Oh, stop with the desperate show of strength. It's getting to be more annoying than funny."

This conversation is more like two people stabbing each other with knives, and watching the carnage, I think:

We're already done for.

The moment the first body showed up, the moment Yuri was killed, we lost the ability to stop *Kingdom Royale.*

All the same...I still can't accept this.

Yuri was the one who said we would be fine as long as we trusted one another. But now, it's her body that's preventing us from doing that. I can't possibly accept such a horrible outcome.

Tears of frustration well up within me. The president's eyes widen as she sees my reaction. As I try my hardest to fight it down, a slender arm wraps around my shoulders.

Long black hair sticks to my cheek, staunching the flow of tears.

"......It's all right, Kazuki."

I know, though. There's no basis for Maria to say that.

"Hoshino." The president says my name. "I like that you're so kind-hearted." She continues in a gentle voice, as if calming a child. "But I won't allow you to use that kindness to hold me back, understand?"

Those words were more than enough to hammer it home: For us, peacetime was over.

▶Day 2 <C> Kazuki Hoshino's Room

No target has been selected for Murder yet.

In the past, that would have been enough to comfort me, but not anymore.

I have no idea who can use the Murder command. But I know whoever it is will undoubtedly be choosing a target.

And I'm sure they will try to force me to kill their victim.

"HeY_hey_hEy_It's_aLMOst_Private_Meeting_timE. ChOose_who_yOU_wouLd_liKE_to_meeT_with."

I quickly touch the name MARIA OTONASHI when it appears with my pointer finger.

"PleAse_waIT_a_biT_until_eVERyone_finishes_chOOsing."

After a clearly longer wait than before, the Private Meeting chart flashes onto the monitor... Someone could be drawing things out on purpose to mess with the order of the meetings.

Iroha Shindo	→	Kazuki Hoshino	3:40 PM – 4:10 PM
~~Yuri Yanagi~~	Dead		
Daiya Oomine	→	Kazuki Hoshino	4:20 PM – 4:50 PM
Kazuki Hoshino	→	Maria Otonashi	3:00 PM – 3:30 PM
Koudai Kamiuchi	→	Daiya Oomine	3:00 PM – 3:30 PM
Maria Otonashi	→	Iroha Shindo	4:20 PM – 4:50 PM

"......"

Daiya and the president have both picked me. Daiya I get, but why would the president chose me?

I think it's possible Daiya is both the Revolutionary and the owner of the Game of Indolence. The idea of another owner is too convenient for me to believe.

...But if Daiya is neither the Revolutionary nor the owner, then both positions would pretty much have to be the president.

Both of the prime suspects are seeking to meet with me.

I shiver as I think back over them at each other's throats in the common area. There's no way I can face off with either of them.

Cradling my head, I wait until it's time to see Maria.

▶Day 2 <C> Private Meeting with Maria Otonashi – Maria Otonashi's Room

Maria sits on her bed, arms folded and face tense.

She starts talking as soon as I sit down next to her.

"Kazuki, we can't allow anyone else to die besides Yanagi. You know that, right?"

"Yeah."

"But that's going to be extremely difficult. The way things are now, the Revolutionary is sure to kill again... We must do something to alter this course of events."

"What can we do...?" I ask.

Maria clenches her jaw hard for a moment before answering.

"I'll tell Shindo everything there is to know about the Game of Indolence."

"Huh...?"

But the president might be the owner.

"I understand your apprehensions. The thing is, the time for avoiding risks is over... I know it may put you in danger, but please forgive me."

"...Were you...keeping quiet about the Boxes until now because you were worried about me?"

"Why else would I?"

Maria furrows her brow as if puzzled.

...I have a few vague thoughts about her decision...but now doesn't seem to be the time to bring them up, so I continue the conversation.

"Well...you're telling the president about Boxes because you assume Daiya is the owner of the Game of Indolence, right?"

"Yes."

"Do you expect her to believe you? The way she is now...don't you think she'll probably just try to kill Daiya...?"

Maria grimaces.

"......Yeah, most likely. Despite that, we absolutely must prove to Shindo and Kamiuchi that there's another way out of *Kingdom Royale* besides winning. I'll have to do everything I can to make sure my intentions get through to them if I want to keep them from killing Daiya... That's going to be easier said than done, though."

"...Oh, but hey, if Daiya is the owner, then the president isn't the Revolutionary, which means she won't be able to do anything about Daiya with Magic. I'm the Sorcerer after all. We're in the clear as long as I don't press the button."

"Why do you think Daiya being the owner indicates that Shindo isn't the Revolutionary?"

"Huh...? Well, if she didn't have a reason to want *Kingdom Royale* to start, she wouldn't have any motivation to kill Yuri, right...?"

Maria doesn't respond affirmatively to my obvious question.

"Daiya gave reasons people could have for killing Yanagi first... But consider this approach. Gaining an advantage in the game didn't matter to them. They simply hated someone so much they wanted them dead, even before this, and that person was Yanagi. *That's why they couldn't help but do it once they found themselves in circumstances where it could be rationalized.*"

"Huh...?"

I'm staring at Maria, wondering if this is one of those occasions where she's joking but doesn't sound like it, but the serious expression never leaves her face.

"...No way. Th-this is Yuri we're talking about, right? No one would ever have it in for her like that."

"Yuri was charming. Charm that sways people's emotions can also stir up negative feelings at times. I'm sure some girls were jealous of Yanagi's popularity with boys, for example. Or maybe she rejected someone, and their love for her turned to hate."

"...But..."

"...Anyway, these are all just possibilities. I didn't notice anything off about Shindo's attitude toward Yanagi, either. Shindo has been blessed with many gifts herself, too. I can't imagine her being jealous of Yanagi. What I'm really trying to say is that it's dangerous to get too invested in a single idea."

That's certainly true. I've only been considering situations where the Revolutionary and the owner are one and the same. I could end up in trouble if I don't take alternatives into account.

What should I do? I don't have any time to think, but the questions keep piling up. I've got to keep believing there is something to be done. I know that, but this situation—it's just hopeless.

"......Kazuki."

I don't realize I've lowered my head until I feel a comfortable weight on it. Maria is mussing my hair with her hand.

"I don't know about Shindo, but I was certainly jealous of Yanagi."

"Huh?"

I instinctively raise my head and look at Maria.

Still rubbing my hair, Maria continues with no particular expression on her face.

"I don't know why, but even though you called me Otonashi for so long, you called her by her first name, Yuri. Yanagi being the way she is, she was acting familiar with you and holding your hand—she even whispered in your ear. And then promising to have a Private Meeting with you? That really ticked me off."

"......?"

"Why do you look so confused?"

"Why would that make you jealous...?"

Maria's hand rubbing my hair suddenly stops.

"...Are you serious?"

"U-uh..."

"All right then, let me lay it out to you plain and simple. What I'm saying is that it upset me to see you attracted to Yanagi."

As she says this, Maria places her hand on top of mine and leans in until her face is inches away. Though I'm used to seeing her now, her features really are beautiful, and I feel my face quickly heating up.

"Um...y-you're a bit...close..."

"Do you know why that Private Meeting would make me angry...? A completely private meeting means that you two, a boy and a girl, would be all alone together."

Maria says this softly by my ear, almost intentionally trying to tickle it with her breath. She then jabs her pointer finger into it.

"Ack!"

Hearing my little yelp, Maria abruptly drops her alluring character, draws the corners of her mouth up into a grin, and begins to laugh. As I sit there perplexed, she steps back and watches me with that big smile on her face.

"You really know how to let younger women mess with you, huh, Kazuki?"

I finally realize she's been teasing me this whole time.

Ngh… I never really thought of Maria as being younger than me…

"Oh, come on, it was just a joke. There's no need to be so flustered."

……What— What part of that was a joke…?

As I sit there silent and gloomy, Maria's grin fades, and she speaks again.

"There's nothing to worry about, Kazuki."

Then she gives me that smile that is kinder than anyone else's.

"I'll protect you."

▶Day 2 <C> Private Meeting with Iroha Shindo – Kazuki Hoshino's Room

"Wh-why…?"

The word escapes my mouth upon my return from Maria's room.

I stare at the monitor dumbfounded.

A TARGET HAS BEEN SELECTED FOR MURDER.

That, I'm okay with. I predicted that whoever could use Murder would put the command into effect. But the person they targeted was not who I expected.

WILL YOU BURN IROHA SHINDO TO DEATH WITH MAGIC?

Under this message is a portrait of the president's face, with the text KILL? over her eyes. If I press this picture, she will be burned to death.

Why has she been targeted for Murder and not Daiya…?

I struggle to get my thoughts under control. The ones who can target someone for Murder are the King or the Double. Neither Maria nor I have those roles. And it's not like the president is going to Murder herself. Which narrows it down to Daiya or Kamiuchi.

...But Kamiuchi is totally dead set on Daiya being the Revolutionary. I can't see why he would choose the president.

So is it Daiya...? No, didn't the president say Daiya isn't the King or the Double?

Hold on a second.

Then who the hell is the Revolutionary...?

"Hey, I'm here."

"Eep!"

It's enough to make me jump.

"Hmm? Aren't you overreacting a bit? You should've known I was coming." The president waves at me from in front of the door with an astonished look on her face.

"S-sorry, President."

"...I'm not going to force you, but would you mind not calling me 'President' anymore? It feels like you're ignoring who I am as an individual, and it kinda bugs me."

"...So, 'Miss Shindo'...?"

"I prefer Iroha."

"...Miss Iroha."

"You can drop the 'Miss,' too... But whatever. I'm going to sit here."

Though she says she isn't going to force me, the president—Iroha—makes her wishes crystal clear, then sits on the table like Daiya did yesterday.

"Um...Iroha, why did you pick to meet with me?"

The president answers my question with a smile.

"To beg for my life."

"......Huh?"

"Don't you get it? If I don't kill Daiya Oomine during <C> today, then I'm pretty much guaranteed to get targeted for Assassinate. In other words, my life is in your hands. Please, oh *please* save me, Kazuki!"

"...Why are you telling me this...?"

"I mean, you're the Sorcerer, aren't you?"

My shock threatens to show itself, so I do my best to fight it down. This is exactly the same trick Daiya pulled on me. Screwing up the same way twice would just be pathetic.

"Darn, he didn't fall for it. You're more on guard than I thought. But anyway, if we don't get Oomine with Murder today, I'm a goner. Why me?!"

"...Um, are you in a position to use Murder?"

"No." Iroha's denial is simple.

"Even if I was the Sorcerer, I wouldn't be able to help you on my own. I can't choose a target for Murder, after all."

"I wonder. Do you really think Kamiuchi and Otonashi wouldn't Murder Daiya Oomine after how our talk went in the commons? He was digging his own grave back there. Don't you think you might be able to affect the outcome if you do something?"

I know Maria at the very least would never choose someone to kill, and the actual target is Iroha herself.

I can't say any of that, though, so I keep my mouth shut.

"The reason why I chose you specifically for a Private Meeting was because, as far as I can tell, you're the one most likely to let Oomine off the hook. It seems like you two knew each other before this, and even if not, well, you're a nice guy."

These words just strike me as sarcasm.

"I'm going to be in trouble if you spare him. So I've come here to give you a bit of encouragement."

Encouragement to kill Daiya...?

"......But you said it yourself, didn't you? If you kill someone, your life will fall apart."

"Yeah, that's true. Suggesting that you murder someone will undoubtedly throw the rest of my life into shambles. I'll be perfectly honest, with as little imagination as I have, it's hard for me to tell just how much suffering it'll bring me. Or maybe I'm just trying to avoid thinking about it. After all—"

Iroha is smiling, but there is a strong gleam in her eye as she finishes.

"—even that is better than dying, no doubt about it."

It finally dawns on me as I see the total resolve and complete lack of hesitation in her eyes.

I see just how dangerous Iroha is.

It isn't just her inborn abilities that makes her superhuman; it's her mental nature. Iroha may be similar to Maria in the way she can plunge headlong toward her goals without getting sidetracked. But unlike Maria, who is able to change her goals because of how she prioritizes others—more than anyone else I know—Iroha prioritizes her own objectives over everything else, and under no circumstances will she change them. And for this reason, from time to time, she'll run right over others. Like a train crushing a pebble on the tracks, she does it naturally, without even noticing.

Right now, her goal happens to be "staying alive."

A chill runs up my spine as I remember how I first met her.

"......Hey," I begin.

Iroha said she wanted me to press the button to kill Daiya. What would happen, though, if I shook my head to her request? What would she do, since she believes she's going to be killed if I don't comply?

"You don't happen to have your knife on you, do you?"

Iroha's eyes go wide. "Well, well." She looks at me with deep interest, then says, *"How did you know?"*

Iroha shoves her hand in her skirt, casually pulls out a knife, and then hurls it into the wall by the door.

"I bet you spotted it trying to get a look at my panties. What a perv."

"......"

"Ha-ha, I'm just joking... Well, I guess carrying around a concealed knife doesn't really qualify as a joke. Aw man... Will you give me a chance to explain myself? I wasn't carrying it because of this Private Meeting with you. I've kept it on me any time I'm not in my own room. That's the truth."

"But you would use the knife to threaten me if I said I wouldn't Murder Daiya, right?"

"I would. But that's normal, isn't it?"

I shake my head at her offhand response. That's far from normal.

"Really? Well, whatever. Now I can't threaten you, though."

"Um, that sack..."

"Huh?"

"The sack on the table has my knife in it, so I need you to hand it to me."

Iroha's eyes go wide for a moment, and then she gives a rueful grin. She sweeps up the whole sack and tosses it over to me.

Taking the sack, I pull out the knife and throw it toward the door just as Iroha did.

"...And did you also sit on the table because you knew my knife would be in here?"

"Ah-ha-ha, I didn't think it through that much, no. More importantly, can I ask you something?"

"Ask me what?"

Iroha looks me dead in the eyes as she says:

"Whether you're going to help kill Daiya Oomine, that's what."

She speaks lightly, with a kind smile on her face.

"......Um..."

"What?"

"I'm not killing anybody. Not Daiya, and not anybody else."

After I reply, Iroha sits there watching me with a smile on her face, not saying anything. I can't help but break eye contact and look down in the face of her silent entreaty.

"You don't get it. This is what I'm asking you."

Iroha pauses for a moment, then continues:

"I'm asking whether you're going to kill Daiya Oomine or kill me."

I raise my head and look at Iroha. She regards me with the kind of expression you'd give a disobedient child.

"Don't make the mistake of thinking you can escape your sins if you don't press the button. If you do, you'll definitely be killing Oomine. But even if you don't, you'll be killing me."

"B-but that's—"

"You're free to think what you want, but that's how I see things. If I get Assassinated, it'll be because you let me die, in my view."

"Ugh..."

I understand that. Once I'm part of this game of murder, there's no longer any way to keep my hands entirely clean.

"...I understand what you're trying to say. But I can't Murder Daiya during today's <C>... I can't explain why, though."

"Are you saying you're a Class that has nothing to do with Murder? ...Or that Oomine really hasn't been chosen as the target?" she asks with an angry scowl.

Of course, I can't answer either question.

"Judging by your face, I'd say it's the latter! Hey! That means I'm definitely gonna die!"

As I remain silent in the face of her misplaced excitement, Iroha sighs and collapses faceup on the table.

She covers her eyes with her arm as if exhausted.

"...Hey, Hoshino."

Then, in a quiet voice, she asks a question on a completely different topic:

"Yuri was cute, wasn't she?"

Unsure of why Iroha is asking this suddenly, I stay quiet and look at her.

"Before I met her, I had never been jealous of anyone. Generally, I thought I could do anything. But even being the way I was, the first time I respected, envied—and yeah, probably felt jealousy toward someone...was Yuri."

Jealousy.

I remember Maria's comment that being charming can elicit negative emotions at times, too.

"I haven't told anyone this because I really hate letting others see my weak side, but in my entire time in high school, I've only liked one boy. We had always gotten along well... But I'm not really smart when it comes to love, see, so I was content to just be friends with him."

Iroha shows me a slightly bitter smile as she speaks.

"That is, until he and Yuri started dating."

I can't read the emotion in her expression.

"They were both friends of mine, so they would both come to me for advice about their relationship. So I even knew how things were progressing—if they held hands, if they kissed, things like that. Hearing all of it made me think—I really wished the whole thing would fall apart."

"......"

"And then, as if my prayers were answered, they broke up after three months. I was so stupid. Yuri and him splitting up didn't mean something good was in store for me. He and I were never going to start a relationship, and it would just alienate me from Yuri instead... So why had I wished for something so meaningless? Basically, all I had wished for was the two of them to be unhappy. Two people who supposedly meant a lot to me. It was horrible of me, and that's putting it mildly."

Iroha eventually looks at me.

"Did you think that was a boring, run-of-the-mill story?"

I shake my head vigorously.

"Well, what it means is that even I worry about such trite things sometimes... Some 'superhuman' I am."

Iroha shifts her gaze up toward the light bulb hanging from the ceiling as she continues:

"...I forgot about all those childish concerns. I really did. All I needed to know was that I loved Yuri."

A self-deprecating smile appears on her face.

"But when Yuri died, I remembered all of it. Like, I couldn't get it out of my head. This pointless memory won't leave my mind. Even though Yuri, who I loved so much, is dead, that stupid stuff is all I can think about."

Iroha slowly turns her head in my direction and looks at me.

"So, Hoshino, what do you think?" Gently, softly, she asks, "Do you think I—*actually liked Yuri*?"

There's nothing I can say about that.

Iroha blankly regards me for a moment as I remain silent. But watching me sit quietly without saying a word, she unexpectedly starts to smile.

"Heh-heh… So? You like my plan?"

"…Huh?"

"Learning about my human side makes you wanna help me out, right?" she says, then starts cackling.

But I understand. She's trying to play it off as some joke or funny story, but I have no doubt that the things she told me were how she really felt. She doesn't have anyone she can show her vulnerabilities to. I'm sure that applies not just to others but also to herself. That's why she doesn't know her own heart.

She was able to express her weakness because she truly feels death bearing down on her.

I've closed my mouth and lowered my eyes, and Iroha stops smiling.

And then, in a humorous tone, she says:

"I've put a curse on you."

Her expression is full of life.

"Now once I die, you're going to remember our talk forever."

Her plan…is a success.

Even if she does turn out to be the mastermind, I still can't find it in me to wish her dead.

▶Day 2 <C> Private Meeting with Daiya Oomine – Kazuki Hoshino's Room

Daiya sits on the table, fiddling with his portable device.

"Did you know, Kazu? Our devices won't work for anyone but their owners," he says, then starts going through my bag on the table. He pulls out my portable device and shows me how he can't use it.

"…You're very calm."

He's the complete opposite of Iroha and her desperation.

"It's because I know I won't be targeted for Murder."

"Huh…?"

Daiya smiles.

"Don't be boring and ask how I know. We're all aware it's because I'm the one who chose the Murder target."

"…So that means you're—"

"I'm the King."

He says it so naturally that I almost take his words at face value—but that's exactly what I shouldn't do. I know this is another one of his tricks.

I rack my brain for an arguable point.

"…Um, if you're the King, then I guess that would mean you know Iroha is the Revolutionary, right? If so, why didn't you pick Iroha right after <C> period started? Why did you choose her after your Private Meeting with Kamiuchi?"

"During <B> period, Shindo did sound like she could be the culprit, but the truth is, I wasn't entirely sure. I was just about as suspicious of Kamiuchi as she was."

"Kamiuchi?"

The Kamiuchi who got so emotional after Yuri's death?

"So you thought his anger was just an act?"

"He's a dangerous guy in his own way. Even you must have felt like he's tricky and hard to pin down, right?"

I give a small nod.

"Try to remember. The first person Shindo picked for a Private Meeting was Kamiuchi. That basically means she was on guard against him more than anyone else."

Iroha *had* chosen Kamiuchi first…

"…By the way, Daiya, I get the feeling you know Kamiuchi from before."

"Yeah, I do. We went to the same middle school. I didn't really remember his face, though."

"……Huh? But Kamiuchi doesn't seem to know you."

"That's probably just because a mere peasant such as myself is beneath the notice of the great Lord Kamiuchi, don't you think? I just have good grades, but he's famous. I could tell you all the juicy rumors I've heard about him, but we don't need to do that now, do we?"

So I guess for the time being, I should take it that Daiya and Iroha had heard enough bad things about Kamiuchi to put them on guard against him.

"Now then, I'm going to share one other extremely interesting tidbit with you."

"...What is it?"

"The Revolutionary didn't want to kill Yanagi."

"...Huh?"

My mouth hangs open.

"Hoo boy... Do I really have to lay everything out for you? The King has another command aside from Murder, you know."

"Ah!"

That's right—he also has Switch Places.

If the King used that command, it could result in Assassinate killing an unintended target.

"The Revolutionary was trying to kill me, not Yanagi."

Daiya had smelled the danger in the air, so he used Switch Places on the first day. That's why Yuri, the Double, had gotten killed instead of him.

If that's true, then it would be hard to say for sure that Kamiuchi's anger was all an act, even if he really is the Revolutionary. After all, it would have been Daiya's fault he killed Yuri, the girl he liked.

"I ascertained during my previous Private Meeting that Kamiuchi isn't the Revolutionary. That means it's impossible for the Revolutionary to be anyone other than Shindo."

If everything Daiya says is true, that would mean Iroha killed Yuri accidentally.

And if that's true...then it slightly changes the meaning of Iroha's confession earlier.

She was forcing herself to find a reason why she had no choice but to kill Yuri so she could rationalize her guilt away.

—That might be one way of interpreting things.

"B-but...if so, then why were you being so vague during <B> period? If you just told us all that you were the King, it could've done away with the suspicion on you, right?"

"Revealing my own Class is about the stupidest plan I've ever heard of."

"But you just told me..."

"That's because I trust that you would never kill me."

"Huh...?"

My eyes go wide, and Daiya scowls as if to say, *Dammit*. He then looks away from me, almost like he's embarrassed.

...Did he say he trusts me? Daiya trusts in something?

"...I'll explain why I said what I did during <B> period."

Daiya launches into his explanation as if his last remark never left his mouth.

"I'll start with my first goal: narrowing down the suspects. If I were the Revolutionary, I would naturally have known that Yanagi died because of Switch Places. I brought up the topic of why anyone would go after Yanagi so I could make the suspect slip up. That ended up failing, though."

I nod and beckon him to keep going.

"And then there's my other intent: to keep people from guessing I'm the King."

"...Why did you need to do that?"

"The Revolutionary made me the scapegoat, namely so that I would be targeted for Murder. But if I'm the King, then that's pointless. Obviously. After all, if I'm the King, then only I can pick who to Murder."

The one who was actually selected for Murder is Iroha and not Daiya.

"So what do you think the Revolutionary would do if I not only didn't work as a scapegoat but was a huge pain, since I was onto their lies?"

Daiya smiles as if this topic is pleasant.

"Kill me with Assassinate."

I gulp audibly.

"That's why it's better to have them suspect as little as possible that I might be the King."

I recall what Iroha said:

"You would have noticed all of this if you were the King or the Double, so I know you aren't either of those Classes. So what does that leave us with?"

Yeah, now I see.

That exchange was meant to make Iroha think he wasn't the King.

"......Oh."

The speed of Daiya's mind threatens to overwhelm me.

But—if it does, then maybe it's okay to go along with what he says. He said he believes in me, and I can't believe he was just acting... Or maybe I just don't want to believe he was.

He's my friend, after all.

Is it all right to trust Daiya? And if Iroha is the Revolutionary, is it also safe to say she's the owner?

"Kazu."

Daiya summons me out of my silence.

"Kill Iroha Shindo."

"—That's…"

"If you use Magic, neither you nor Otonashi will have any more dangerous bridges to cross, and you can find the solution to this Box. All it takes is one little act of determination on your part to free yourself from everything. No, you have to kill her. Are you prepared to let my resolve go to waste?"

I know that the suggestion Daiya cut me off with is the smart answer.

But…

"I won't use Magic."

That answer won't change.

"If you're saying Iroha is the owner, then I'll find some way to persuade her to reveal the Box."

"Even though your hesitation may end up killing you and Otonashi?"

"That's right."

Daiya snorts in derision at my quick declaration.

"I commend you on keeping up your patented 'good boy' act even in a killing game. Guess you're planning to have faith in her being a good person, too? That's about the worst case of sugarcoating I've ever seen. Take a look at my arms. Your rotten values have given me goose bumps so big I could use my skin as a washboard. What're you going to do about that?"

"…Sorry."

For some reason I apologize, even though I'm the one being slandered here. But…I don't know, it just feels like another one of those back-and-forths we always have in class.

"But I knew all that," Daiya says, pointedly rubbing his arm. "I knew what you'd probably say." He has a resigned smirk on his face.

"…Heh-heh."

"You freak me out. How the hell is your brain wired that you laugh when someone's making fun of you?"

Come on, though. It's so totally Daiya to show me respect while he's insulting me.

And that's when I become certain.

Daiya is telling the truth.

▶Day 2 <D> The Common Area

The Revolutionary—and the owner of the Game of Indolence—is Iroha Shindo.

That's the conclusion I've reached. I have to find some way to get through to her and keep her from doing anything else crazy.

It should be possible. She's not such a horrible person to just totally disregard the lives of others, after all. That's why there has to be some way out of this, no matter how difficult it may seem.

Or so I thought.

How could I have been so incredibly naive?

"Ah— Aaaaah..."

Someone is gasping.

A red puddle grows, threating to reach my feet. I stand rooted in place, not even thinking of avoiding it.

"Kamiuchi!"

Maria's yell snaps me back to my senses. I realize what exactly it is at my feet.

"Ah—"

That spreading red puddle...is blood.

I know that. I understand. But I'm trying not to process why it keeps growing and growing, growing and growing and growing and growing and growing and growing.

I slowly kneel down and gently touch the face near my feet. I'm answered with an almost teasing smile.

That expression is so typical for the one making it that I can't help but say the name:

"......*Iroha.*"

Splish, splish, splish...

What's that sound?

Splish. It's footsteps. Each step leaves a red footprint on the floor. *Splish, splish.* The guy making that sound goes and sits in a chair as if nothing has happened at all.

Even though he plunged a knife into Iroha.

"Kamiuchi, why...?"

"Why? Hoshino, you sure do say some funny things. I did it because if I left her alive, she would've killed us all. Naturally, I had to stop her, right?"

"But there could've been another way..."

I stop short in the middle of what I was going to say.

Kamiuchi's hands are shaking hard. He, too, notices this almost ridiculous level of trembling and suddenly begins giggling ("Heh...heh-heh-heh...") in a way that's completely inappropriate for the situation.

I'm sure Kamiuchi learned in his Private Meeting with Daiya that Iroha was the Revolutionary, and he got it into his head that he'd be killed if he didn't do something.

But to think that would drive him straight to violence... Ah, now I get it. Daiya and Iroha were right to be on guard against him.

"Ungh...," she moans.

Maria, who had been standing somewhere in a daze, snaps out of it and rushes over to Iroha. She begins looking over her body, trying to find a way to treat her—

—and then steps away without saying a single word.

"......I see. A scapegoat...," Iroha says, then with a big cough, spits up some blood. "Whoa, I'm coughing up blood... I really screwed up... How lame...," she whispers in a nearly inaudible voice.

"......"

I can't say anything.

Even though there's a woman coughing up blood in front of me, dying before me, I think:

This might be for the best.

"I'm sorry." Iroha's eyes close... She's too weak to keep them open any longer. "......I'm sorry for cursing you...as I planned."

In a small voice, as if mustering the last of her strength, she struggles to say:

"...I'm sorry I couldn't save you."

"—What?"

Those are her final words.

She's sorry she couldn't save me?

I continue staring at her motionless form as I come to grasp the meaning of her words.

Iroha knew there was someone dangerous among us who would

murder Yuri without a second thought. Knowing this, she had no choice but to kill that person.

She took the forefront in *Kingdom Royale*, a game where the more you stand out, the more suspicious you are. With her strong sense of responsibility, she did this to turn the situation in a better direction, regardless of the danger she was placing herself in.

—She was prepared to let her life fall into ruin.

To protect her own life.

To protect all our lives.

"......Ah."

I reach down and touch her face once more.

But she doesn't show me that teasing smile again.

She's motionless. Not breathing. Not alive.

And despite this, the Game of Indolence has not ended.

"......"

I stand up.

Slowly, so slowly, I turn my head to look at him.

Daiya Oomine is touching the earrings in his right ear with a blank expression on his face.

•Iroha Shindo, dead via stab wound to the chest inflicted by Koudai Kamiuchi

▶Day 2 <E> Kazuki Hoshino's Room

KOUDAI KAMIUCHI WAS STRANGLED TO DEATH BY ASSASSINATE.

Now there is no one left to challenge him.

•Koudai Kamiuchi, dead via Assassinate

▶Day 3 <B> The Common Area

"The game was decided the moment I realized you're the Sorcerer."

With just three of us left in the common area, Daiya begins telling us all his tricks.

Maria sits in her chair, looking haggard. Since she knew everything, she had tried her hardest to explain to Kamiuchi about Boxes, but he refused to hear any of it.

And then, Koudai Kamiuchi was killed.

In the end, we couldn't do anything to prevent his death.

Why did I believe Daiya? Why did I fall for such a convenient lie like the existence of another suspect, even though I knew he was the owner?

I knew *Kingdom Royale* was a game of deceive or be deceived…

That's why I also understand how it's my fault things ended up this way. But still…

"You said you trusted me."

Daiya smirks at my caustic remark. "Yeah, I did. I said I trusted that there was no way you could kill me."

"…And that was all just talk so that you could fool me."

"That was a slip of the tongue. If you were smart, you might've noticed the real implications."

I scowl.

"Still don't get it? I assumed there was no way you could kill me as the Sorcerer. What I'm saying is, *I was making fun of you because you can't off me, no matter how far I take this.*"

I bite my lip.

…So basically, he was mocking me. I thought he looked away from me then because he was embarrassed, but the truth is that he was actually just flustered because of his little verbal slipup.

"As the Revolutionary, naturally I'm going to want to know who the Sorcerer is, since they would be another Class with the ability to kill."

"That's why you asked if I was the Sorcerer…"

He wasn't concerned about me; he merely wanted to know who the most dangerous Class was.

"And then you were. So if I let you live, I would never be a candidate for Murder." Daiya smirks, then says, *"Because I trust you."*

So that's why Daiya said the game was over the moment he figured out I was the Sorcerer…

"Still, even you might have used Magic if you were absolutely sure I was the Revolutionary. And even if you didn't, you might have tried something else. So all I needed to do was convince you I wasn't the Revolutionary."

I fell for Daiya's scheme and ended up believing Iroha was the Revolutionary. Damn, it really was that simple.

All along, what I should have done was what I talked about with Maria back when all this started. I should have found a way to get through to Daiya and get him to hand over the Box.

It only seemed complicated because Daiya made it appear to be.

"...Even then, not everything went smoothly. Yanagi in particular."

"Yuri?"

"Yeah. She was trying to recruit other people as allies. She probably would have been able to get everyone on her side except for me. If that had happened, things wouldn't have worked out this way."

...I see. Daiya wanted the game to start, and the presence of someone trying to stop *Kingdom Royale* was a thorn in his side. That was why he shot down her plan to share all our Classes, and why he killed her first.

"Now, then—"

Daiya brings his explanation to an end.

Letting out a breath, he looks over at Maria in her chair.

"All I need to do is kill one more person, and then it's game over."

The Revolutionary has one enemy left.

Maria Otonashi, the Prince.

She doesn't even raise her head at the proclamation of her death.

...Ah, I see now.

The Revolutionary has no need to kill the Sorcerer to win. That's why I'll survive. Maria can save my life without lifting a finger. *And Maria seems to have absolutely no interest in her own life.*

So she couldn't care less about *Kingdom Royale.*

She's saying it's fine, and she doesn't mind if she's killed.

"......"

Like hell.

I can't let this happen.

If Maria says she's a Box, and she's willing to disregard that and offer her life up to save mine, then...

"Daiya."

...naturally, *I have to reject that.*

I don't mince words as I fix Daiya with a glare.

"I will never, ever allow you to kill Maria."

That's right. Back when Maria realized she's powerless in this Box, didn't she say she thought I might have to do something? Now that time has come.

At the time, I didn't know what I should do. But now…

"If you're intending to kill Maria, then I'll stop you. I'll do whatever it takes. Even if it means—"

The conclusion leaves my mouth so easily.

"—killing you, Daiya."

Maria hadn't even twitched at Daiya's intent to kill her, but my words make her open her eyes and look my way.

I'm sorry, Maria. I'm betraying your faith in me, that I could never kill someone.

"…You sound like you mean it," Daiya says, then falls silent.

He once said it himself: If I'm certain who the Revolutionary is, there's a possibility I would use Magic.

He failed. Kamiuchi went against Daiya's predictions and killed Iroha, which means he doesn't have any more scapegoats. It's now obvious he is the Revolutionary.

"Give us the Box, Daiya. Do that, and you don't have to die," I say.

Daiya's expression seems to suggest he still has it all under control. But as someone who *used to be* his friend, I know better.

He's more panicked than ever.

"I don't have to die, eh?" Going back over my words quietly, Daiya sneers. "…Kazu, do you know what type of Box the Game of Indolence is?"

I frown at this sudden change of topic.

"The Game of Indolence is a Box that staves off boredom by forcing the summoned players into a killing game called *Kingdom Royale.*"

"…So what's your point?"

"Do you really think the ultimate escape from tedium would just end like this? Do you think I'd actually be satisfied with a single playthrough of the game?"

"……"

"This is meaningless slaughter. Your desire to save Otonashi, your resolve to kill me if that's what it takes to do so—all of it is pointless. In the end, none of it matters. The next game will have different players, and that alone will make it unfold differently. You and I may even end up working together."

What the hell is he talking about...?

"That said, the sins you commit in this stupid game will carry over, if nothing else. If you kill me, that guilt will remain with you."

"...So you're saying I shouldn't kill you?"

"Yeah."

...Oh, come on.

I had thought it might be something more, but it's all just a bunch of garbage meant to try to save his life. Even now, Daiya's still trying to pull the wool over my eyes.

"I didn't want to see you reduced to this, Daiya. I don't care about any of that, so just hand over the Box."

As a former friend of mine, Daiya has to know—more than he probably cares to admit—that I am seriously prepared to kill him.

Even so...

"That's the one thing I cannot do." Daiya states this coldly.

"...You know you have nowhere else to turn, right?"

"Like I give a crap. I know about the hope the Boxes bring. And now that I do, I'm not gonna let anyone take that away from me. If I lose my Box, then I'll no longer have any purpose. I'd just be a CO_2 factory blundering through the motions of life in a thoughtless haze."

"The Boxes are hope...?"

The Boxes that brought such suffering to Mogi, to Asami, to Miyazaki...?

"They aren't as good as you think."

"Shut up. You annoy me. I'm not interested in your cheap-ass bargain bin values."

Scarily enough, Daiya sounds like he really means it. He's serious when he says the Box is his hope. Even though he knows well enough about the previous two instances.

As my thoughts reach this point, I suddenly realize something. *Could it be...?*

"Does this have something to do with Kokone?"

Daiya doesn't respond right away.

"...Does what have something to do with her?"

"I mean, does Kokone have something to do with your wish?"

"Why're you bringing her up? I almost feel sorry for your pitiful brain and the irrelevant intellectual disasters it comes up with."

I don't miss it, though. There was a stony expression on Daiya's face before he said that, and he seemed to be forcing himself.

No doubt about it. Kokone definitely has some connection to Daiya's wish.

I'm certain of it now.

"You...aren't going to hand over the Box, are you?"

I'm certain—that Daiya will not part with the Box, no matter what.

"Uh, yeah. That's what I said, right?"

No matter how much I threaten to kill him, Daiya will never give us the Box. In other words, Daiya has us—

"......"

Realizing this, I look at Maria.

Maria is smiling.

"......Stop it."

She's smiling... As if she has given up on everything.

But maybe that's an appropriate reaction to our situation.

I've known it all along. I can never kill Daiya and crush the Box by force. I can never use Magic, no matter the circumstances.

Not because I don't have the resolve to kill Daiya. My willpower doesn't have anything to do with it. I mean, I can't use Magic on my own. Yeah—

I can't use Magic because Maria will absolutely never take another person's life.

And that's why...

...we are going to lose to Daiya Oomine.

▶Day 3 <C> Private Meeting with Maria Otonashi – Maria Otonashi's Room

I knew it would be this way, but for the entire thirty minutes, Maria ignored my pleas for us to use Murder.

I think back on what Maria said yesterday.

"I will protect you."

I took her words at face value.

I had been a fool basking in her strength and kindness, taking it for granted.

Even though I knew the truth. Even though I was well aware that *Kingdom Royale* was a game of murder and deception, and Maria was powerless within it.

I was wrong.

I'm the one who should have said those words.

"I will protect you, Maria."

But it's too late, and there's no time left.

▶Day 3 <E> Kazuki Hoshino's Room

MARIA OTONASHI WAS STRANGLED TO DEATH BY ASSASSINATE.

•Maria Otonashi, dead via Assassinate

************ **GAME OVER** ************

• Winners

Daiya Oomine (Player)

The Revolutionary; survived and killed Yuri Yanagi, Koudai Kamiuchi, and Maria Otonashi via Assassinate.

*Victory conditions were fulfilled by the deaths of Yuri Yanagi, Koudai Kamiuchi, and Maria Otonashi.

Kazuki Hoshino

The Sorcerer; survived.

*Victory conditions were fulfilled by skillfully surviving.

• Losers

Iroha Shindo

The Knight; died due to hemorrhagic shock after being stabbed in the chest with a knife by Koudai Kamiuchi on the second day.

Yuri Yanagi

The Double; died via Daiya Oomine's Assassinate on the first day.

Koudai Kamiuchi

The King; killed Iroha Shindo by hand on the second day. Died via Daiya Oomine's Assassinate on the same day.

Maria Otonashi

The Prince; died via Daiya Oomine's Assassinate on the third day.

Kazuki Hoshino

Maria Otonashi

Iroha Shindo

Yuri Yanagi

Koudai Kamiuchi

Daiya Oomine

START GAME

▶Day 1 <A> Kazuki Hoshino's Room

I wake up with a start in unfamiliar surroundings, my eyes falling upon a naked light bulb and a bare concrete ceiling.

"...What is this room?"

Why am I here all of a sudden?

I can feel myself about to lose it, so I review what I can remember of what happened.

I'm sure I was sleeping on my bottom bunk. I don't remember moving from there. *I don't remember leaving or meeting anyone, either.*

I survey the room, I check the contents of the hemp sack, and then the rules of the killing game are explained to me by a green bear—Noitan—that appears with a "Good_morning."

This is the work of a Box.

That's why Maria is here.

▶Day 1 <B> The Common Area

The view changes instantly.

First off, it's white. Unnaturally so, like a newly built hospital without doctors or nurses or patients.

I spot him, the closest one to me.

"...Daiya."

"Long time no see, Kazu."

Daiya, who had disappeared without a trace, greets me with perfect ease, as if we were just bumping into each other in the classroom for the first time in a while after summer break came to an end.

Even though I'm still unsure how to react, Daiya continues on.

"You should thank me, Kazu. I stopped things from getting violent."

Daiya jabs his thumb at a girl with midlength hair.

"This girl was gonna push you down and threaten you with a knife."

"What...?!"

Eyes wide, I look at her. That green bear had said we would be killing one another, so does this mean it's about to get started...?

"Hold on there, Oomine. He's going to get the wrong idea if you put it that way," the girl counters. I've heard her voice somewhere before.

"Wrong idea? Nothing I said was incorrect."

"Shut up. The only thing that isn't mistaken here is your obvious bad intentions. I only did it because I thought it was a necessary measure."

I realize I've actually heard her voice often, through a microphone. Right, she's the student council president.

"A necessary measure, huh? Fine, but if you keep doing stuff like that, you're just going to invite extra mistrust and put yourself at a disadvantage, you know? If you're scared, you should just try trembling like you're supposed to."

The president seems a bit surprised by Daiya's words. "...Yeah, well. Putting on a strong front is a bad habit of mine."

Is she saying she's worried despite acting so levelheaded...? Uh, she has to be joking, right?

"If you want to learn to express your fear naturally, take a look at that girl clinging to you and follow her example."

The shoulders of the girl with black hair next to the president jump so hard I almost feel bad for her. The president pats the girl's hair as if to reassure her it'll be okay.

...Her face really is pure white. Nothing's even happened; isn't she a little too terrified?

But—there is something kinda cute about her.

I realize thinking along those lines is unwise, and I may not be as nervous as I should be, but I can't fight this protective urge welling up within me, like the way you'd react to seeing a small animal.

It's an appeal Maria doesn't have.

"Kazuki."

"—Urk!"

Th-that's right. I knew she'd be here, but I got careless.

"What was that weird yelp for?"

"I-it's nothing, Maria."

I escape her suspicious gaze by turning my face.

"Whatever... You do know what kind of situation we're in, though? I'm shocked you aren't more on edge from how abnormal this all is..."

"S-sorry."

"This isn't the time or place to fall for a girl."

"......"

Guess she really did catch me staring at the black-haired girl.

As I stand there quietly refusing to meet her gaze, Maria removes one of her loafers and presses the sole against the side of my face. *That hurts, you know. Plus, it's dirty.*

Shoe still pressed to my face, Maria whispers in my ear:

"You know there's a Box at work here, right...?"

...Yeah, she's right.

This situation can't be anything other than a Box. That means this is Daiya's handiwork.

Still, I'm acting like I've never even heard of a Box before.

"Yo... Hey, do I spy three pretty girls? Lucky me!"

There are six chairs, and the sixth player arrives.

Now all the participants in the killing game Noitan described are here.

The brown-haired student, who was the last to join us and still seems somewhat unsure of how things are unfolding, suggests we introduce ourselves, and we promptly do.

The boy with brown hair is Koudai Kamiuchi. The girl who was apparently going to pull a knife on me is Iroha Shindo, our student council president. And the black-haired girl is—

"—Yuri Yanagi."

* * *

The name alone is enough to make my thoughts pause in their tracks.

"......Huh? Uh, ah, did I say something strange?"

"I-it's nothing. I just— I have a friend with the same last name is all."

She looks dubiously at me as I wave my hands frantically, then asks, "A friend?"

"U-um..."

I try to remember that person—

"—Ah."

Unexpectedly, something resurfaces in my mind. Namely, what Daiya said to me in the cafeteria.

"It's because you want to keep seeking. Hmph, even if I accept what you're saying for the sake of argument, that still brings up another question. Why have you become like that?"

I get it now. The one I couldn't see through the fog back then—

"......My classmate from when I was in middle school."

Nana Yanagi.

As her name leaps back into my mind unbidden, I shake my head furiously. I don't want to remember her. I once hoped she would remain forgotten.

Yanagi, the first girl I fell in love with.

"A classmate? Well, maybe you feel some connection with me because of that, then?"

Yanagi—no, that's a bit confusing, so Yuri—says this with her head inclined to one side.

"Huh? Oh y-yeah... It'd be nice if we hit it off right away."

Yuri smiles charmingly... She really is too cute.

"What're you in such good spirits for, Kazuki?"

My shoulders tense up, and I turn around, only to see Maria giving me a reproachful look.

"I-I'm not in good spirits."

"No, you definitely are. You have that happy expression guys get when they talk to a pretty girl. You look all weak and sappy."

"You're a pretty girl, too."

"......Are you trying to flatter me? I hope you don't think that'll work on me."

As we go on like this for a bit, Yuri eventually steps in.

"U-um...I'm not that pretty, you know...?"

"That's not true. I think you're really beautiful."

"O-oh..."

Yuri has turned bright red. As I gaze into her face, unable to understand why, I feel a sudden impact on the back of my head.

"O-ow!"

Turning around, I see Kamiuchi staring at his own fist.

"???"

"Uh, I saw you and got super-PO'd, so I guess I just kinda did it without thinking. My bad."

As I stand there holding my head, still clueless as to what's going on, Maria sighs.

"Who'd have thought it'd take a natural-born skirt-chaser to ease the tension."

"...That's mean."

"Whatever. It'll be easier for us all to talk this way. Let's get down to business."

And with that, Maria pins Daiya with a hard stare.

"What's the meaning of all this, Daiya Oomine?"

The somewhat relaxed atmosphere disperses.

All of our attention turns to Daiya when he's singled out. Instead of being taken aback at the suspicion, he flashes a brazen grin.

"......Huh?" Yuri gasps, apparently not completely following the situation. "Is this...something Oomine did...?"

"What I'm about to say might sound bizarre, but will you try to believe it?"

Yuri is still blinking at Maria's words. The president speaks up in her place.

"Aw... Sorry, Otonashi, but we'll decide for ourselves what we want to believe. Don't try to force anything on us."

"Fair enough. But I still have to say it. This is the kind of subject you have to ask people to believe before bringing it up."

The president pouts, then nods as if to say, *I see.*

"Okay, I guess I'll start by explaining just what a Box is. Now, here's the thing about Boxes—"

With the introduction, Maria begins describing Boxes to everyone.

They exist to grant wishes. They're the reason why we're involved in this situation. Three of us already know about them. And Daiya Oomine is the owner of the Game of Indolence.

Everyone listens to the explanation earnestly.

"...That all sounds really messed up."

The president has a stern look on her face, just as she had the whole time while she was listening to Maria.

"So the Boxes themselves are really messed up, but the situation we're in now is plenty crazy, too. It doesn't even sound too far-fetched that such a thing could exist."

"So does that mean you believe us?" I ask.

The president pouts again, as if it's a habit of hers.

"...No, I'm just saying I wouldn't be too surprised if something like that existed. I mean, even I could cook up some ridiculous reasons for a ridiculous situation, you know?"

"I see...," I reply, crestfallen.

The president scratches her head and continues on.

"...But, well, I think if you were truly trying to deceive us, you would tell a more realistic lie. You answered all our questions straightaway, and you almost went out of your way to say some things that were fishy... Hmm, I'd say it's about fifty-fifty for me... Hey, what do you think, Kamiuchi?"

"I don't think I can buy it." Kamiuchi flat-out rejects our explanation. "It isn't so much what they're saying—more like it's a little odd that the three of them are working together. They all knew one another before this, right?"

"B-but we haven't had any time to put our heads together and conspire on this..." I counter his argument feebly.

"I hear ya. But you still knew each from before, so weren't you just going along with what Maricchi was saying? Not to mention the worst-case scenario, where all three of you are behind this whole thing, you know?"

"That's not true!"

"Hoshino, please don't get so worked up. What I'm trying to say is, it's not easy to trust the opinions of three people who seem to be in cahoots," Kamiuchi says.

The president agrees. "He's got something there."

"How about you, Yuri?"

"...Um, sorry, but...I just can't make myself believe in the idea of these Boxes. I'm sorry."

She doesn't speak haltingly because she lacks confidence in her own ideas, but more likely because she isn't used to expressing negative opinions.

"Hey, Yuri, you must've taken my side because you want to get in good with me, huh?"

"Uh...? N-no, that's not it..."

"Hee-hee, it's so cute how that little joke was enough to make you blush bright red!"

The president butts in as if to protect Yuri, who is turning an even deeper shade of crimson. "Okay, okay, stop teasing Yuri."

"President, maybe you're just jealous because the guys don't make passes at you like they do Yuri here?"

"It wouldn't count if someone like you hit on me."

"Ouch! You're so mean. You might be surprised, but I've got a lot of fans among the ladies."

The president sighs, as if to say she is through listening to him, and gets the conversation back on track.

"Anyway, can we set the matter of the Boxes aside for now? Yuri, Kamiuchi, I'd also like to ask the two of you to not dismiss the possibility so easily and just keep the idea in the back of your minds. If you do, then maybe down the line when it's time to decide whether to believe in them, you can be a bit more objective."

The two of them nod sincerely at her idea.

Maria says, "I guess I can live with that," although her dissatisfied expression contradicts her words.

...Well, I feel the same way. It's disappointing that we can't get them to believe us about the Boxes, but on the other hand, there's not much we can do about it.

"...President, what can we do to persuade you of this...?"

She replies to my timid query straightaway. "You have to prove with actions that you are trustworthy. If you do, even if we don't buy into the idea of the Boxes, we'll be likely to go along with your suggestions on how to get out of this mess."

Easier said than done.

"Um, what exactly do we need to...?"

My question is interrupted.

"HeY_hey_hey. It_sounds_like_yOU_alL_are_taLKing_about_something_disturbing. BuT_I'll_teLL_you_aBOut_someTHing_rEAL_thAT_blowS_that_out_of_the_wATEr."

"AnYWaY_I_wish_you_all_GOOd_luck. DoN'T_let_the_game_end_with_some_bORIng_outCOme_where_YoU_are_all_muMMIfied."

After he finishes explaining the rules of *Kingdom Royale*, Noitan vanishes.

"Hey, Otonashi."

The president seems to have changed her demeanor somewhat after hearing such awful things.

"If what you're saying is true, there's a way for us all to survive aside from completing *Kingdom Royale*, right?"

"Yeah."

Maria's firm assertion seems to resonate even more deeply with the president.

...Maybe this could lead them to believe us even more quickly than expected.

I mean, the president—and the others, too—they don't want to take part in this killing game. If we keep fumbling along without a clue and time starts running out, someone will end up breaking. Then the game would begin. We need to act before that happens.

That's why, if we can establish another option for getting out of this, they'll most likely jump at the chance.

"Shall I tell you exactly what it is?" And Maria can tell them.

"...Okay, I'll bite. What do we need to do?"

"If we can get Daiya to take out his Box, we will be free."

Everyone's eyes turn to Daiya instantly at her words. Seeing our attitudes, he clicks his tongue in annoyance and makes sure it's loud enough for us all to hear.

"Hey, Daiya, aren't you going respond to Maria?"

Rejecting the president's question, Daiya turns away and stays silent.

"...To be honest, if you're gonna call Oomine suspicious, I won't object," Kamiuchi says with a bit of a chill in his voice, as if he's irritated. He then turns around and smiles at Yuri. "Of course, you're on the same page as me, right, Yuri?"

"Huh?!"

Yuri's eyes grow huge as she is suddenly dragged into the fray.

"Th-that's... I never..."

She's fumbling over her words, but judging by the way she keeps peeking over at Daiya, I'd have to say she agrees with Kamiuchi.

The atmosphere of the situation is now completely to Daiya's disadvantage.

"Ugh..." He reacts to this whole affair with a deep sigh. "You idiots are all a bunch of puppets."

But not even his insults are enough to change the mood.

"How about you try defending yourself before you start calling people idiots?" the president replies calmly.

Daiya gives an icy laugh as if thoroughly disgusted.

"...What? What's with the unpleasant laughter?" she asks.

"You believe others so readily—I was just thinking how easy it would be for all of you to get wiped out. And you say you're all honor students? You've gotta be kidding me."

"Stop with the smoke and mirrors, Daiya. Hurry up and state your case."

"Sorry, but I'll save that until after the Private Meetings."

"Huh? What sort of weak attitude is that? Aren't you just buying time to come up with a good explanation?"

"I can't decide what stance to take, and there's someone I want to confer with."

"Okay, but you're overwhelmingly suspicious right now. Are you fine with that?"

Daiya doesn't say anything in response.

▶Day 1 <C> Kazuki Hoshino's Room

YOUR CLASS IS THE REVOLUTIONARY.

I stand in place for a moment, taking in the message.

"......Huh?"

I'm the Revolutionary? The Revolutionary, as in the most indisputably dangerous Class...?

If *Kingdom Royale* starts, everyone is going to come after me straight off the bat, no doubt about it. No matter how you slice it, the Revolutionary and his ability to take lives independently are a hazard.

...Wait, let's try looking at it from another angle.

If I'm the Revolutionary, then that means I won't get hit with Assassinate. If you put it that way, I'm actually in a pretty safe position.

And that's not all. Since I'm the Revolutionary, the one most likely to kick *Kingdom Royale* into motion, I can keep the game from starting.

So I should assume I'm in relatively little danger, yeah.

Telling myself this, I let out a deep breath and try to calm my racing heart.

"HeY_hey_hEy_Kazuki_iT'S_tiME_for_the Private Meetings."

"Eep!"

As usual, the mascot appears at the worst possible timing for my heart. I'm positive he's doing it on purpose.

I listen to Noitan's explanation of the Private Meetings, and then, of course, I choose Maria.

Iroha Shindo	→	Koudai Kamiuchi	3:40 PM – 4:10 PM
Yuri Yanagi	→	Iroha Shindo	4:20 PM – 4:50 PM
Daiya Oomine	→	Kazuki Hoshino	3:40 PM – 4:10 PM
Kazuki Hoshino	→	Maria Otonashi	3:00 PM – 3:30 PM
Koudai Kamiuchi	→	Yuri Yanagi	3:00 PM – 3:30 PM
Maria Otonashi	→	Daiya Oomine	4:20 PM – 4:50 PM

"...Daiya chose me?"

Does that mean I'm the one Daiya wanted to confer with?

......At any rate, I'll have time to speak with Maria before that.

▶Day 1 <C> Private Meeting with Maria Otonashi – Maria Otonashi's Room

"We might've had a bit of unexpected luck there."

Maria says this out of nowhere.

"...What're you talking about?"

"Telling them about Boxes."

"...Huh? Is there a situation where we wouldn't be able to?"

"There is. If we did it after we learned the rules of the game, the others would most likely think we were spreading disinformation in an attempt to win. We were able to talk about it because they would seriously consider the existence of Boxes in those circumstances."

She might just be right.

"Thanks to that, we have a chance of victory. As time runs out, they'll have no choice but to trust in us since we have the only plan for getting out of this. Oomine will probably be difficult as we saw earlier, but that's just the way he is, so they won't trust him."

I think that's true. I feel bad about it, but when it comes down to trusting us or Daiya, probably no one would take his side.

"...Maria."

"What is it?"

"Is Daiya really the owner of the Box?"

Maria furrows her brows.

"In light of our situation, I don't see any other possibility, do you?"

"But you could also say it was Daiya who kept things from getting out of control by stopping the president. Thanks to that, we had a good environment for the president and the rest to hear us out about the Boxes. Do you really think he would have done that if he wanted *Kingdom Royale* to start?"

"...What you say is true. But I'm guessing he probably wasn't thinking that far ahead. Or maybe he wants us to think that so we'll drop our guard or something."

"Hmm."

"You're free to worry over whatever you want, but we know Daiya is the owner. Do you have any better evidence?"

"...You're right."

"Now that we're in agreement there, let's go over things. We need to get Daiya to bring out the Box. We have to convince him to do this. But he isn't going to respond to our attempts easily."

I nod dutifully. Yeah, our real work has just begun.

"We need to make time to get through to Daiya. To that end, we have to make sure *Kingdom Royale* never gets started, even if just by accident."

"How do we do that?"

"Build a relationship of trust, as Shindo said. A good starting point would be to have those who actually have the ability to kill, particularly the Revolutionary, come forward and reveal themselves, but..."

"Oh, I'm the Revolutionary."

"Really?!"

"Y-yeah."

Maria's enthusiasm throws me off a bit as I answer.

"This is huge. It means there's no chance the Revolutionary will be consumed by paranoia and commit an error. Then, if we wait for the right moment and have you reveal yourself, there won't be any better way to win their trust."

...So it really is a good thing I'm the Revolutionary.

"So what's your Class, Maria?"

"I'm the Double."

"...Oh."

According to the game, that makes us enemies.

"Our chances are good. All that leaves... Yeah, the one possibility that bothers me is that Daiya might conspire with someone to use Magic behind the scenes."

"I have a Private Meeting with Daiya, so I'll try asking him a few things then... Um, should I try driving the point home about not starting *Kingdom Royale*?"

"...Yeah. But be very careful. One slipup, and he could deduce that you're the Revolutionary."

▶Day 1 <C> Private Meeting with Daiya Oomine – Kazuki Hoshino's Room

"I have no intention of playing a crappy game like Kingdom Royale."

That's the first thing Daiya says as he enters my room.

"What're you all goggle-eyed for?"

"I...I mean—"

Is it really possible Daiya, the owner, wouldn't want to play his own game?

"The look on your face says you don't understand where I'm coming from."

He's right on the money, so I can't say anything.

"The answer to that question is simple: I'm not the owner of this shitty Box. Forcing people into a game where they kill one another? Heh-heh... Sounds pretty unproductive to me. It has no reason to exist."

"...I...think the same..."

"So is your insistence that I'm the creator of this Box some roundabout way of insulting me?"

"Uh, no…"

So maybe this is what Daiya is trying to say: He's without a doubt an owner. But the Box that makes people play *Kingdom Royale* is not his.

This Box has another owner.

"That aside, what's with this Box? I can't sense any way of interfering with it. If it doesn't have any loose ends, whoever made it must really know what they're doing."

"Huh…?"

"Come on, why are you so astonished? Think about it. Otonashi can detect Boxes, interfere with them, and knows about O because she's an owner, right? I'm an owner now, too, so it shouldn't surprise you that I can do all that."

"That's true…"

"What's with that face? From where I stand, you're the strange one since you know about O even though you're supposed to forget completely about them."

"…But that's—"

"Yeah, it's not possible. We're owners, and it's possible for us to do these things, since we can consciously make use of our special nature. But you're not an owner, are you?"

I don't have anything to say to that.

"…So what is it that makes Box owners different, exactly?"

Daiya crosses his arms and thinks a moment before answering my question.

"…This is just the way I see it, but from the moment a person comes into possession of a Box, they're no longer human, because the Box allows them to surpass the limitations of humanity. *When they step outside the bounds of these limitations, owners step outside the bounds of normal life.* That's what makes them special."

I frown as if I have no idea what he means, and Daiya continues his explanation.

"Leaving your original standpoint allows you to perceive things you never could before. I don't mean that we can see Boxes or O in the visual sense, but more that *we are just aware of them.* Like how you'll spot a salon you've passed by many times, but only when you need to get your hair cut."

...I guess Daiya thought that would help me understand.

"So why is it that you can perceive O?" he asks.

"I don't know." My reply is a little apathetic.

"...Hey, Kazu, you rejected it, but apparently, you did touch a Box once."

Not really wanting to answer fully, I simply give a tiny nod.

"That's because you truly felt that a wish-granting Box sounded like a bunch of nonsense. *You knew there were no limitations.* Back then, you took a step outside the norm—how does that sound?"

"How does it sound...? So does that mean there's no going back for anyone who has ever been an owner? Mogi doesn't remember O at all."

"Yeah, I guess there is that. Mogi and Asami both got really lucky in that sense. They thought of their Boxes as something special. *They didn't notice the true nature of the Boxes.* That's why they could go back to how they once were, and why they couldn't use their Boxes fully."

Daiya looks me over.

"But I get the feeling you could master a Box. That's why you ended up like this just by touching one."

"No way. I'm normal."

"No, I'm afraid you're not. I said it before, but you're floating in suspension. Away from normal life."

"You're wrong."

"I'm not. On the contrary, you were abnormal even before you came into contact with a Box. You were, in essence, very close to the nature of an owner from the very beginning. No... Maybe less an owner and closer to O."

"—Stop it!!" I yell. I can never accept the idea that I resemble that disgusting being in any way.

Daiya observes my exclamation. After a moment, he sighs.

"Well, there's not much point in talking about this now. All I wanted to do was get you to trust that I'm not the owner of this Box."

"...I...don't think I can believe that anymore."

"Hey, don't make up your mind so quickly. Say...would you believe me if I could stop *Kingdom Royale* in its tracks?"

"...What do you mean?"

"If *Kingdom Royale* is designed to make people kill and deceive one another, then all we have to do is lead it in a direction where that doesn't happen. Do that, and the game doesn't work anymore."

...It seems to be in line with our goal of keeping *Kingdom Royale* from starting...*I guess?*

"Do you think the owner of this Box would want the game to stop running?"

"No, I don't think so... Uh, hold on. Do you have an actual plan for how to stop *Kingdom Royale?*"

"Yeah."

That's when Daiya says it.

"Find the Revolutionary."

"......"

I instinctively swallow.

I fight down the urge to let my panic show on my face. That was close. He almost outed me as the Revolutionary.

"Why will finding the Revolutionary stop the game?"

I manage to ask the question naturally. Daiya replies, without the slightest hint of doubt toward me.

"Because the game will never start if they don't use Assassinate. If we can find the Revolutionary and threaten them so they can't use Assassinate, then we've achieved our objective."

The word "threaten" scares me a bit, but I maintain my composure and raise another question.

"How would we keep them from using that ability...?"

"There are plenty of ways. For instance, we could say that if they kill anyone, we'll out them as the Revolutionary. Once exposed, the Revolutionary has no chance of victory. No one's dumb enough to kill someone for no reason."

"But let's say we find the Revolutionary and prevent them from using Assassinate. Then what about Magic...? Wouldn't it still be possible for the game to start if someone dies that way?"

"There's no worry of that." Daiya denies it firmly.

"Why?"

"Because I'm the Sorcerer."

...Huh? Is he really okay with just revealing his Class to me like that?

"R-really...? You aren't just trying to fool me?"

"Does it benefit me in this game to lie to you about being the Sorcerer here?"

"That's—"

I think for a moment, but I can't come up with anything.

"All I want is to get out of this worthless Box. By necessity, I have to work with you and Otonashi to do that. That's why I don't mind telling you my Class."

"...Are you sure? We might be Classes that are opposed to each other..."

"Do the Classes of this game matter to you? You know we can resolve all of this if we destroy the Box, after all."

...He might be right.

"All I want is for you and Otonashi to realize I am not the owner of this Box... In light of that, I need to ask you something."

Daiya casually says his question:

"You're the Revolutionary, aren't you?"

My reaction allows Daiya to ascertain my Class beyond a shadow of a doubt. It seems he was already pretty certain who I was from my response when he said we need to find the Revolutionary.

That's how I ended up under Daiya's control.

But...I don't think there's any way around it. I'm positive none of the others would've been able to keep their Class hidden from him, either.

▶Day 1 <D> The Common Area

Daiya's claim that he wants to stop *Kingdom Royale* from functioning could be true.

"If you all don't want to murder one another, then we should all come out in the open about our Classes."

That's his proposal, after all. If we all tell one another our Classes, then no one can lie. Furthermore, the Class Daiya would reveal is the Sorcerer, one that's capable of killing.

"...Is that the conclusion you reached after consulting with Hoshino?" In the end, it's the president who breaks the lengthy silence.

"Yeah. I don't feel like playing along with this game."

"That's all well and good. But I wonder if that's true? This is just an example, but—"

"Let me just say this: I'll assume that anyone who doesn't go along with this plan intends on playing *Kingdom Royale*."

"You can't just say that."

"Can't I? I'm the only one who gets to decide how I judge things," Daiya retorts.

The president scowls.

"B-but, Iroha, I was thinking of suggesting exactly the same idea," Yuri says.

"...Yeah, I kinda sensed that during our Private Meeting."

The president looks around at all of us, then asks, "Are we all fine with this? If you have any objections, speak up."

No one says a thing. I had thought Kamiuchi might object, since this is Daiya's plan, but he doesn't give a peep. Maybe because Yuri agrees with it.

"Ugh... Seriously?" the president complains. "Well, guess I can't very well go against it and be the odd one out..."

"So you're for revealing our Classes?"

"Yeah, yeah."

Once the president gives up, Daiya hands us each a piece of notebook paper from his hemp sack.

"Write down your Class on these. I only have one pen, so we'll have to take turns. Make sure no one sees you while you're writing so there won't be any cheating. Once you're done, put your paper facedown. Then, once I give the signal, we'll all flip them over at the same time."

Daiya writes first, and then we all write our Classes as directed: Maria, followed by me, the president, Yuri, and Kamiuchi. There are now six pieces of paper facedown on the table.

"All right, show 'em."

Everyone turns over their paper. I read the Class on each one.

Maria is the Double.

The president is the King.

Yuri is the Prince.

Kamiuchi is the Knight.

And then Daiya—who I had thought might pull something—is the Sorcerer, just as he claimed.

"...So Hoshino is the Revolutionary... Phew, that's a bit of a relief. I don't know what I would've done if it was Kamiuchi."

"Hang on there, President—what's that supposed to mean?!"

"Um, yeah. Exactly what I said."

Kamiuchi grimaces with a "Whoa!"

"How about it, Your Presidency?" Daiya asks. "Seems like just the type of outcome to put you at ease, eh?"

"...Yeah. Unless Hoshino is secretly some scheming bastard, then I guess I'm okay with it."

"...Hey, come on."

Daiya ignores my pouting and continues, "I also have one more proposal. I want to collect all the knives we were given. This won't entirely prevent violence, but it's still safer than the alternative."

"Don't tell me you're trying to hoard all the knives for yourself, Oomine?" Kamiuchi says. "In that case, I'm against it. It's way too dangerous to leave all that power in your hands."

"Hmph, well then, how about we gather them all in someone else's room?"

The president cuts in. "How about Yuri's or Hoshino's rooms? They seem like the most valid choices. Anyway, I'm fine with either one, so how about you two work it out?"

"Huh?" "Huh?"

The two of us, who were just picked, exclaim at the same time and look at each other.

"Oh, go ahead, Hoshino."

"Oh, it's okay. Why don't you do it, Yuri?"

"I couldn't..."

"I couldn't, either..."

"I think you would keep the knives stored safe and sound, Hoshino, so..."

"I'd feel safer if it was you, Yuri."

"But..."

"You'd just be holding on to them."

"But it'd be the same if they were with you—"

"Okay, okay, the knives go with Yuri." The president stops our conversation with a clap of her hands, then settles the matter herself.

"I-Iroha."

"Pipe down, it's settled! Each of us will bring our knives tomorrow during <B>. Yuri will then collect them. How does that sound? Satisfied now, Oomine?"

"Not yet."

The president lets out a breath at Daiya's statement. "Okay, your imperial majesty, what shall we do next?"

Daiya carries on, completely disregarding the president's sarcasm. "We've stopped *Kingdom Royale* temporarily. But our objective isn't just to stop it, but to escape it altogether. All we did now was reach a preliminary agreement. If the situation changes, that won't hold true any longer."

"Yeah, I guess I can see that. So what, then? Does that mean you know something especially vital?"

"I know a way to get us out of the game."

The president and the rest of us freeze at his retort.

...Daiya, you can't mea—

"We just need to destroy the Box."

He really did it. He acknowledged the existence of Boxes in front of the others.

Even though he is currently the prime suspect.

"Boxes do indeed exist, as Maria Otonashi said. If you can't believe that, then just think of the Box as an analogy for whatever forced us into this mess. At any rate, in order to accomplish our goal, we need to destroy this Box. And we can do this by killing the owner, or the one in possession of the Box."

"But didn't Otonashi basically say you were the owner?"

"...I'm going to retract that estimation for the time being." Maria jumps into the conversation with a stern face. "This doesn't change the fact that Oomine is my prime suspect. I've just concluded that a decision would be a little premature. I felt this during my Private Meeting just now, and the plan Oomine proposed will undoubtedly prevent any killing... That's why I can't be certain Oomine is the owner."

The president tilts her head in obvious puzzlement at Maria's unexpected assistance. Neither I nor Maria is sure how much of what Daiya's saying is sincere. We don't know what his aims are for us.

Still, there's no mistaking the truth that *Kingdom Royale* is the work of a Box.

If we can just get everyone to believe that, then the game will not start. And then, we can work as one and find a solution to—

* * *

"Oh, give me a break."

My optimistic thoughts come to a screeching halt.

Everyone focuses on Kamiuchi, the source of the outburst.

"Why are you even seriously considering this, President? There's no need to think about any of it."

"...Why is that?"

Kamiuchi flashes a condescending smile at the president's question, then bluntly replies:

"I mean—*the three of them are totally in cahoots, right?*"

I'm...chilled to the bone.

There isn't a trace of his usual flippancy on his face. Instead, it's blank, with a hint of something hard and cold lurking underneath.

"This is just a trap. None of us has any idea what type of person would be an owner, right? That's why if we start searching for this owner, we'd have no choice but to follow these three in everything during our hunt. Do you know what that means?"

Kamiuchi continues with a thin smile.

"These guys—*can set somebody up as the owner we have to kill.*"

What—

What is he saying...?

"We have no intention of killing the owner—"

"—Shut up."

A single sentence. That's all it takes to create an enormous impact.

I'm instantly aware of something. This person is—different. From an unknown world. And his world—contains violence.

Not one of us is able to open our mouth.

The long silence is finally broken as Kamiuchi lets out a deep exhalation. He breathes several times, in-out, in-out, and he's wearing his usual clownish expression.

But it's impossible to see it the same way as before.

"You can't believe all this Box crap, either, can you, Yuri?"

Yuri gulps audibly.

He's forcing her to take his side. He won't allow any dissenting opinions.

"......I, um..."

He's trying to get Yuri to agree with him. By doing so, he can establish a false rationale for rejecting our ideas.

That's his aim.

If Yuri agrees with him, we're done for.

But it's no good. As weak willed as she is, Yuri isn't capable of rejecting him the way he is now.

With tears in her eyes, Yuri looks at me for a moment before averting her gaze.

Then, with trembling lips, she whispers:

"......No, I can't believe it."

Yep, we're screwed.

Or so I thought. But then—

"...But..."

—she keeps speaking.

"...at the very least, I think I can trust Hoshino. So the idea that he would be trying to trap us...is something I...can't accept."

She can't accept it.

She said it clearly. She was trembling and scared, but she still managed to push Kamiuchi's opinion to the side and defend me.

Maybe because she had to summon so much bravery, Yuri ducks down on the spot, places her hands over her chest, and lets out a ragged breath.

Kamiuchi regards her with wide eyes, probably because he never expected her to refute him. He then directs a piercing gaze toward me. I swallow hard, feeling exactly like a criminal about to be sentenced by a judge.

"Well, I can also acknowledge that Hoshino here seems like an upstanding guy."

Only then does the hostility disappear from his features.

...Did we ride it out...?

Yuri raises her face and looks at me. Her tense face relaxes, and she smiles.

That's how, thanks to Yuri's bravery, we were able to hold on to some hope of finding a resolution.

Daiya, the president, Kamiuchi, and Maria all return to their own rooms. Just as I'm about to follow them through the door, Yuri grabs my hand.

"What's up?"

I notice it as soon as the words leave my mouth. Her hand is shaking.

"...I was...scared." She murmurs this, not raising her head. "That guy... terrified me."

"Yeah... But...you really helped us all. Thank you."

I smile at Yuri to reassure her, but her face remains as frightened as before.

"My Private Meeting."

"...Huh?"

"I'm scared of my next Private Meeting...with that guy." Yuri's complexion is as white as it was when I first saw her.

"I-it'll be okay. Kamiuchi seems to like you, so I'm sure—"

"—That's why I'm scared!!"

She looks up and raises her voice enough to startle me. She looks down again, embarrassed at her loud exclamation.

"S-sorry for losing my composure."

"I-it's okay..."

What's this all about?

In the Private Meetings, we're alone with the other person in our cell-like rooms. Kamiuchi has a thing for Yuri, so I can't imagine he would kill her, but—

"Oh..."

The realization hits me.

I know exactly what Yuri is so afraid of.

I think she sees I've caught her meaning, because she grips me tight.

"......I really meant it, you know?"

"Huh?"

"I didn't say I could trust you earlier because I wanted Kamiuchi to back down. I said it because I meant it."

Her trembling grows even more intense. I'm getting worried, so I peer into her downturned face.

"I'm scared... So scared."

Yuri is crying.

What do I do? What am I supposed to do here?

This isn't the type of situation I can think my way through, so for the time being I just squeeze her shaky hand in reply.

Yuri places her left hand over mine and grips me even tighter.

"Oh..."

Again.

It's happening again.

I'm remembering, again.

I remember Nana Yanagi even more vividly than I did when I heard Yuri's name.

In fact, how could I have forgotten her so completely? It hasn't even been two years, but recently, her existence hadn't crossed my mind at all. I had blocked her out of my thoughts like none of it had ever happened.

Could it be that my wish to forget Nana Yanagi, the wish I had been praying for from the moment I betrayed her, had actually been granted?

It had—*by completely blotting it out with mundanity.*

"On the contrary, you were abnormal even before you came into contact with a Box."

That doesn't matter. It has nothing to do with it.

"...I'm sorry, Hoshino, I'm sorry... I'm going to say something selfish, but please forgive me. I trust you, of my own volition. That's why I ask—"

She says it. *Yanagi says it.*

"That's why I ask—please don't betray me."

The tearful entreaty on her face...for some reason it resembles her, my first love.

And then, the moment I think it, the words leave my mouth.

"I won't. I won't betray your trust again, Yanagi."

▶Day 1 <E> Kazuki Hoshino's Room

Upon returning to my room, I reflect on my memories of her.

Nana Yanagi. She was my classmate, the first girl I fell for, and—in a relationship with my best friend.

She and Yuri share the same last name, and they are at once alike and completely different. In a word, she was a troublemaker. She would suddenly shave off her eyebrows with a razor during break, cover the whole classroom in the pink powder of a fire extinguisher—the list of strange things she did was endless. The other girls even started calling her "Ex-ko" behind her back. (The "Ex" was short for "Eccentric.")

I thought Yanagi was scary, and to be honest, I didn't want to have anything to do with her. It would take a rare person to want to associate with a classmate who had bleached-blond hair, wore a decidedly unmodern long skirt that was too much for even the other bad girls, and smoked cigarettes in secret.

But as it happened, I knew just such an oddball.

Toji Kijima, my best friend.

Toji was full of curiosity, and his eyes positively shone whenever he encountered something new. Yanagi's eccentric behavior never failed to ignite that gleam. I think becoming interested in her was an extremely natural thing for Toji. At first, Yanagi rebuffed his advances. But I think the truth is she most likely wanted someone to pay attention to her. She accepted Toji, and they started dating.

Almost as soon as they did, she revealed her true colors.

The true colors—of a deeply lonely girl.

She was dependent on Toji. The extent of her need was, in a word, horrible. She never left his side for even a moment and lashed out at any girls who approached Toji to make them keep their distance. Because Toji wanted her to, she changed her blond hair back to black, wore a normal-length skirt, and buried her cigarettes in the garden.

Toji was everything to Yanagi.

Since he was her world, she couldn't bear it if he said or did anything she didn't like. Even the most trivial remark or behavior hurt her terribly. On occasion, she would even cut her wrists.

The only one who would listen to her at those painful times…was me.

The phone calls I got from her always started with sobbing. She would often drag me off somewhere away from prying eyes during breaks at school, then unleash a flood of tears.

At first, I was just trying to lend her an ear. But as time went on, she began to seek further comfort from me. She would get me to stroke her head, hold her, sleep beside her, even lick up the tears running down her cheeks. I remember her saying some really messed up things, like how the sight of my face as I guiltily lapped up her tears relaxed her.

That's right. In the end, she was dependent on me, too.

Honestly, it was exhausting. I didn't like the way she led me around by the nose, and at times, I even avoided her calls.

And that wasn't just me. I soon found out how sick of it Toji was, too.

After countless talks of splitting up, the two of them finally called it quits for good.

From that time onward, I had to deal with her each and every day. Most people will probably never know what another person's tears taste like, but I licked up so many that I could hardly stand the salty flavor anymore. Even then, I knew I was the only one she had, so I put up with it.

I still had my limits, though. The pent-up anger was beginning to make my stomach hurt. I lost my appetite. I grew irritable. Why was I stuck comforting her when we weren't even lovers?

That's why, one day, I said something about it to her.

"I can't see you anymore."

She didn't understand.

In order to understand my own resolve, I gradually said harsher and harsher things.

I can't see you anymore, you're nothing but trouble, think of someone else for a change, Toji dumped you because you don't think about how other people feel, I can't stand it anymore, quit stalking me, freaking Ex-ko—

Then, the very same day I showered her with abuse—*Yanagi and Toji disappeared.*

The classmates who knew them only while they were together came up with all sorts of stories, like maybe they'd eloped, but I knew that wasn't possible.

So why did they both vanish at the same time?

There was only one answer. Succumbing to hopelessness after I stabbed her in the back, Yanagi called Toji to meet her. And then—she made it so he couldn't come back.

I blamed myself. It was my fault. It was all because I couldn't support her enough. Because I shoved her away, even though I was the one person she could depend on.

But what took over my heart even more than guilt was emptiness.

Each day felt entirely void of meaning. Each day was as flavorless as a piece of gum that's been chewed for three days straight. I found it was missing something. The world lacked flavor.

It lacked that intense, salty flavor.

You're awful. How could you even consider disappearing from my life over a few words like that? Don't you think you can keep depending on me? You— You're so irresponsible, letting me experience that taste and then disappearing.

Why...did it have to be Toji?

If it were me, if you had me, I would have given you everything. I already pretty much had.

Once I reached that point, when I finally realized that my heart had become hollow...I truly, finally understood.

Yeah... What can I say?

I...loved Nana Yanagi.

By the time I realized that, she was already gone. She ran off with Toji, ran off with most of my heart, and vanished.

But though I may have betrayed someone I love, hurt them, drove them into a corner, or killed them, my normal life persisted. I was alive, so I had to keep on living. I had to make a normal world without her in it.

That's why I had to forget her.

I had to forget about Nana Yanagi. She was never the type who would have anything to do with me anyway. I had to seal her away, this eccentric symbol of abnormality.

That's how I was able to truly forget about her, to an almost incredible extent.

Now that I think about it, when did I become so fixated on normality?

CHOOSE THE TARGET YOU WOULD LIKE TO ASSASSINATE.

This message appears on the monitor alongside pictures of all six players, including me.

I can't possibly make a choice like this.

I don't understand the Game of Indolence. I suspect it might not have any meaning behind it at all.

I collapse on my bed.

But what am I trying to do by saying this Box is meaningless? Am I trying to suggest that the normal life I would go back to does have meaning?

That normal life built entirely around forgetting her?

"......"

I think about Yuri. No one needs to point it out—I'm aware that "Nana Yanagi" and "Yuri Yanagi" are beginning to overlap in my mind.

If I can save Yuri without betraying her, maybe I can escape from the spell Nana has on me?

I don't know. I don't know, but—

—the moment Yuri's face surfaces in my mind—
—I taste someone's tears in my parched throat.

▶Day 6 <B> The Common Area

We reach the sixth day without any major developments.

As Daiya had planned, we revealed everyone's Classes and even collected all the knives, bringing *Kingdom Royale* to a halt. Despite this, the other three remain on the fence about Boxes no matter how much we explain to them, so we're stuck when it comes to identifying the owner… And the time limit is approaching fast.

I head from my room to the common area. By this point, I'm completely used to the warping phenomenon that occurs when I go into a new room and don't think anything of it.

A room that is whiter than any naturally occurring shade.

…But whatever. As long as I'm the Revolutionary and Daiya is the Sorcerer, *Kingdom Royale* will never start.

"Kazuki."

As she spots me, Yuri marches swiftly up to me with a little grin on her face.

"Huh? Did something good happen?"

As I say this, Yuri mutters "Huh?" in a small voice and tilts her head, as if she wasn't aware of what she was doing. Watching us from the corner of her eye, Iroha chimes in.

"Yuri's just happy to see you for the first time in a day. She's really grown fond of you."

By her tone, it's hard to tell whether she's joking or serious. Yuri's face blushes a deep red.

"I-Iroha! Quit talking about me like I'm some sort of puppy!"

I imagine Yuri with a dog's tail, wagging as she comes up to me.

"Ha!"

Oh man, that's a great image!

"Wh-why did you laugh just now, Kazuki?!"

She puffs out her cheeks… I've got to find a way to pass off that laugh as something else.

All the same—I really have grown used to talking to these two.

Ever since the second day, we've all made an effort to actively talk to one another to build trust. I've had Private Meetings with everyone. Even Daiya has been cooperative, so the strategy has proven effective.

At the very least, I can no longer imagine any one of us killing someone else.

"...Kazuki, as punishment for laughing, you have to choose me...for a Private Meeting during <C>," Yuri says for some reason, her puffed-out cheeks turning slightly red.

"Fine, but how is that punishment?"

"...Huh? ...Um, w-well, it just is! ...Probably!" Yuri says, flapping her arms with gusto. It's kinda funny.

"Huh?"

Maria, who has been eyeing Yuri, comes over, scratching her head irritably.

"...Huh? What's up, Maria?"

For whatever reason, Maria stays silent, unwilling to open her mouth.

"...To put it this way...you've already had Private Meetings with Yanagi four times, correct?"

"Huh?"

"If you go again today, that'll make it five. I wouldn't be surprised if the others see that as you focusing on one person. Having Private Meetings with a specific person five times may endanger the sense of cooperation we've worked so hard to build among the six of us."

"...Um? So you're saying I shouldn't have a Private Meeting with Yuri; is that right?"

"I'm not saying just with Yuri. I'm saying it's dangerous to be perceived as favoring a specific person."

"...Aren't you overthinking it a bit?"

"You've only had Private Meetings with me three times."

I feel like I'm missing something...

"Otonashi's jealous. How cute," Iroha says with an amused look on her face.

"...Don't get started with that stupid, baseless conjecture. I'm just warning Kazuki about his behavior."

"You're really desperate."

"...You aren't listening to me."

"Maria, are you jealous?" I ask.

Thud!

"O-ow!"

She kicked me in the shin really hard!

"Sigh..."

Kamiuchi, who was watching this exchange and fiddling with his portable device, jumps in disgustedly. "Aw man, I'm so jealous here. I kinda just wish you'd curl up and die, Hoshino."

"Huh? What's to be jealous of...? I just got kicked."

"...What're you playing dumb for? Is that what they call the confidence of the victor?"

When I tilt my head, Kamiuchi lets out a sigh and goes back to messing around with his device.

Despite how it may seem, Kamiuchi and I have gotten pretty used to each other, too. I wasn't sure how things would go the first time I saw that violent side of him, but in speaking with him, I've found him to be surprisingly easy to talk to.

"Huh? Ah, I get it."

Kamiuchi sets his device on the table and stands up.

"What's up?"

"Oh, I was just going back over some past statements and I reached a conclusion."

Kamiuchi walks over to where Daiya is sitting and pats him on the shoulder. Daiya scowls, as if he's annoyed by the overly familiar treatment. This has been happening pretty reliably between these two the last few days.

"Daiya. I'm gonna believe you, about the Box, I mean."

Startled, I ask, "Huh? Really, Kamiuchi?"

"There's no reason to lie, right? ...I mean, at this point it doesn't really matter whether I believe you. With us running short on time, I have to pick one or the other. There aren't any other answers besides the Box, so I don't really have any choice."

Now that he mentions it, Maria did say they wouldn't have any choice but to trust us once time grew short.

"So what was it we needed to do again? I'm pretty sure you said this situation would be fixed if we smash the Box. If that's the case, let's just do this."

With that, Kamiuchi lifts his button-down shirt.

"Let's kill Daiya here."

* * *

"—Huh?"

But there wasn't enough time.

There wasn't time for me to comprehend what he meant.

Before I can even think, he brings down the —

And he kills Daiya.

"……Ah…"

……Huh? What is this…?

Though I can explain what happened, my ability to understand it is far slower.

Kamiuchi slashed Daiya's neck open. Blood sprays from his neck, and he falls silent with his eyes still open. And then—he dies. I can tell that much. But while I can recognize the facts as facts, I cannot assign any meaning to them.

That's why I just stand there, dumbfounded.

Kamiuchi's shirt is now bright red, and his face is wet and crimson with the sticky spray of blood. In his hands is a knife, which he should not have. It's one of the combat weapons we supposedly collected from everyone.

"That's funny," Kamiuchi mutters as he plays with the knife he had concealed underneath his belt. "Wasn't everything supposed to be fixed once the owner dies? And wasn't the owner Daiya here?"

He looks at Maria.

"Hey, that was the story, right, Maricchi?"

Maria is stunned, her eyes wide.

Kamiuchi keeps talking, as if he was never really looking for a response to begin with.

"Maybe it's just that Daiya isn't dead yet? Okay, let's try this."

And with that—

—he plunges the knife into Daiya's neck again.

Blood flows everywhere.

The impact knocks Daiya's body forward, and his head slams into the table with a loud bang. Red liquid spreads across the table.

"Ah…"

Yuri shrieks and falls on her backside.

"Aaaaaaaaaaaaaaaaaaaaaaaaaaaaaaaaaaaaaaah!!"

Kamiuchi looks at her, and his cheeks soften in a smile.

"Your scream is so cute, Yuri... But he sure looks dead to me. Guess that means all that stuff Maricchi said about Boxes in the beginning was either a mistake or BS, huh? Oh, I think I did choose to believe in Boxes, didn't I? Guess I should just assume that Daiya here was a miss."

Kamiuchi says a "miss."

I don't get what he means right away. But before long, I do.

"Maricchi."

The murderer asks his question:

"Who should I try next?"

He's asking who'll be a "hit."

By chance, I notice the hand gripping the knife is shaking.

At first, I think maybe it's in fear of what he has just done. I understand once I see his face, though.

His hand is shaking with excitement.

Ahhh—what a mistake I had made. How did I ever expect to get along with a murderer like this?

He's just been waiting for the right time to unleash the violent nature he's kept hidden away.

Kingdom Royale is a game of killing and deception.

We were unable to stop it. Daiya's experiment was a failure, with the price being his life.

Kingdom Royale started that very first day.

"Why do you...still have a knife?" I ask as I stare at the knife with Daiya's blood still dripping from it.

"Is that really your first question? ...Fine, I'll humor you. Yuri gave me plenty of openings when I went to her room for a Private Meeting, so I took one. That's all."

"...Huh? So it's...my...fault...?"

Yuri looks up and turns her wide eyes on Kamiuchi. The murderer smiles at Yuri, then speaks.

"You gotta be more careful."

"Ah..."

She's rendered speechless, and her tears overflow.

"So, Maricchi, who's next? ...Hey, she's still frozen. Don't you think you're overreacting a bit? Whatever, I still think your naïveté is damn adorable."

Kamiuchi gazes at the blood-soaked knife as he offers his meaningless compliment.

"...I've decided," he says, walking up to me. "Maybe I'll go with Hoshino here, since he's just making me green with envy. I want him dead anyway."

He picks me, in the same tone someone would choose their lunch from a menu.

But in his eyes, there is genuine malicious intent.

I lock up when I see the bloody knife in his hands. It's the same weapon that killed Daiya.

The murderer comes closer.

"Wait."

Kamiuchi stops easily at Maria's voice. "What is it, Maricchi?"

She speaks to the boy with a lust for blood in his eyes.

"I'm an owner."

Kamiuchi narrows his eyes at her words.

"I'm saying you should kill me, not Kazuki."

He seems to have grasped her meaning. He smirks, seemingly by reflex. "Ha-ha, are you saying you want to take his place and save his life? You're really something."

"I'm simply stating the truth," Maria says, glaring at him.

Kamiuchi quickly strides up to her, still holding the knife. Maria raises both of her hands, all but declaring she has no intention of fighting back.

"M-Maria..."

She smiles at me as I call out her name. Seeing the kindness in her face, I'm certain of something.

Maria didn't say that because she has some sort of plan. She really is just prepared to die in my place.

"I'm impressed with you, Maricchi. I never thought I'd meet someone who honestly values the lives of others over their own. They say love's one hell of a drug; maybe they're onto something. This is true love if I've ever seen it."

Maria smiles icily. "Is that so? Well, I'm glad you're impressed."

"Are you really okay with dying just to help Hoshino?"

"Yeah."

Kamiuchi sighs at Maria's direct, unhesitant response. "Well, damn. This love of yours is just too beautiful. Okay, fine. It's not like I want to be the bad guy; I'm just trying get out of here as quick as I can. But I'm not gonna be some cheap-ass villain who just goes 'If that's how you want it, then die' and slices you up. So I'm letting you both off the hook."

Koudai Kamiuchi runs his hands through Maria's hair intimately as he continues:

"You just have to sleep with me, Maricchi."

He presses the knife to her throat with his right hand.

"......"

Maria's face twists with loathing. She glares at Koudai Kamiuchi, then slaps away the hand stroking her hair, even though she's at knifepoint.

"......Shut the hell up. I'd rather die than give my body over to you."

"Ooh, so mean. There are plenty of girls out there lining up to get with me, you know. So you aren't going to accept the offer?"

"Of course not!!"

"All righty, then."

He gives up that easily—or so it seems.

"I'll take Yuri instead."

As if that would ever happen.

He said it with a smile, but his eyes are cold and full of lust; realizing he isn't joking in the slightest, Yuri turns as white as a sheet.

"N-no—!!"

"It doesn't matter if you say no, Yuri, my dear. Maricchi turned me down. Oh, but I like you better anyway, so I'm totally cool with it."

"I—I could never do that..."

"Okay, then I'll kill both Maricchi and Hoshino."

All Yuri can do is blanch another shade whiter in the face of this inhuman statement.

"If you don't want to have the deaths of these two hanging over your head because you told me no, then you should just go along with it."

Yuri slowly turns back and looks at me. Tears stream from her eyes. She can't speak, but her gaze tells me what she wants to say.

"—Please don't betray me."

...Yeah, I see it now. This is the situation Yuri was afraid of from day one. And I made a promise. I promised I wouldn't betray *Yanagi* again.

But even so, if I try to save Yuri now, then Maria will—

"...Stop."

The one who speaks up in a small voice is Maria, not me.

A grin spreads across Koudai Kamiuchi's face as he hears this.

"Hmm? If you've decided you want to play nice with me, then I guess that's okay."

I'm sure she knew he would say this.

Maria bites down hard on her lip, so hard that blood begins flowing from it. She looks away from me—and then says it clearly.

".........Yeah, you'll have to make do with me."

...What...

...What are you saying, Maria?

"Huh? Are you serious?"

Koudai Kamiuchi's eyes are huge.

"......Heh...heh-heh, ah-ha-ha-ha-ha!"

That resolve—

She would rather die than do this, and yet Maria has the resolve to do it, all to save Yuri... Koudai Kamiuchi points at her and laughs.

"Ah-ha-ha-ha-ha-ha! Seriously? I can get why you'd do anything to save your lover boy Hoshino. But you'd really do that for someone like Yuri after only a few days with her? Ah-ha-ha, that is too funny!"

"......What's so funny about it?"

"I mean, talk about culture shock! What the hell kinda values do you have? Putting others before yourself like that is just twisted, if you ask me! Do you really think there's something beautiful in doing that?!"

I'll admit that I can't really relate to Maria's stance on this, either. She neglects her own needs to a fault and occasionally even scoffs at me for caring about her. I can't really say her attitude is entirely about living for others.

But...

...even if that stance is a bit mistaken—

—there is no way I can let someone like him mock it.

"The suffering of others bothers you more than your own? Well then, I take back what I just said. I won't let you take her place. I'm gonna have my way with Yuri no matter what you do."

"...What...are you saying, you bastard?! What's the meaning in that?!"

"It's just more fun."

Even Maria is speechless. Koudai Kamiuchi laughs contemptuously at her shock.

He's toying with her. He's decided her bravery is pathetic, and he's entertaining himself by watching her.

I can't allow this to happen. I'll never allow Koudai Kamiuchi to get away with demeaning Maria's pride like this… I won't allow it, but—

I won't allow it, but why—?

"Ugh…uh…uuuuuuu…"

The sound of Yuri's sobs fills the room. Maria is being held at knifepoint.

Why can't I do anything about it?

"You guys still don't wanna die, right?"

None of us respond, so Koudai Kamiuchi lays it out.

"All right then, from now on, all of you are my slaves."

•Daiya Oomine, dead via slit carotid artery inflicted by Koudai Kamiuchi

▶Day 6 <C> Kazuki Hoshino's Room

"ChoOSE_wHo_you_woULD_likE_to_haVe_a_Private_Meeting_wiTh."

Noitan speaks to me, but I feel to powerless to move.

I couldn't do anything. Maria and Yuri were both suffering, but I couldn't even lift a finger to help them.

Yuri has been forced to pick Koudai Kamiuchi as her choice for her Private Meeting.

Even though she knows what's going to happen to her, she has to pick him. I can only imagine the pain she must be going through…

"—Damn!!"

I bite down on my lip.

I should have been cleverer about this. Even if I couldn't do anything earlier, if I had only given more thought to how dangerous Koudai Kamiuchi was beforehand, none of this would have happened.

Yeah, if I had just come up with some contingency when Yuri came crying to me because she was frightened of him, then things wouldn't have come to this. This is what I get for underestimating *Kingdom Royale* and wasting our time.

…Still, that doesn't mean we're finished yet.

I'm about to press the button for YURI YANAGI when—

"You've only had Private Meetings with me three times."

For some reason, Maria's comment pops into my head.

...Why would I remember her saying that now? That has nothing to do with this. The best option here is obviously to do what I can for Yuri in her time of suffering.

I know Maria's in danger, too. She's also been coerced into choosing Koudai Kamiuchi.

In her case, though, it isn't for the same reasons as Yuri; it's an attempt to prevent us from conferring with each other. His ultimate goal is to survive, so he's trying to crush any chances we might have of conspiring and coming up with a plan to beat him.

It's possible he doesn't even care about the owner anymore. Rather than finding and killing an owner we aren't even sure exists, he's instead focusing on winning *Kingdom Royale.*

Koudai Kamiuchi is the Knight. In order to win, he needs to kill the King and the Prince.

The King he needs dead is Iroha. The Prince is Yuri.

Maria is still in a safer position than the two of them. There's no denying she's in danger, but the level of the threat is markedly different.

That's why—

That's why I choose—*Yuri Yanagi.*

Iroha Shindo	→	Yuri Yanagi	5:00 PM – 5:30 PM
Yuri Yanagi	→	Koudai Kamiuchi	3:00 PM – 4:00 PM
~~Daiya Oomine~~	Dead		
Kazuki Hoshino	→	Yuri Yanagi	4:20 PM – 4:50 PM
Koudai Kamiuchi	→	Yuri Yanagi	3:00 PM – 4:00 PM
Maria Otonashi	→	Koudai Kamiuchi	4:20 PM – 4:50 PM

▶Day 6 <C> Private Meeting with Yuri Yanagi – Yuri Yanagi's Room

Yuri embraces me tight as soon as I enter her room.

I'm sure she's burying her face in my chest because she doesn't want me to see her expression. I caught a glimpse of it as she ran up to me. It was hollow.

"......I didn't want to die," she says this in an empty voice, her face still pressed against me. "No matter what, I didn't want to die. That's why, so I..."

I wrap my arms around her hunched back, not wanting her to say any more.

"U-uuuuuuu..."

She's crying.

Yanagi is crying.

Yeah—could I be any more selfish?

Even now, when I need to show support to Yuri, all I can think about is Yanagi.

It's just that she forced me into this situation so many times back then, listening to the sobs of a girl crying in my arms—

—and so that emotion I had no choice but to experience is playing tricks on me.

It's as if those feelings I once held for Nana Yanagi are back.

Aw, those tears are soaking into her school uniform. What a waste.

I wish I could drink them.

"......"

I hate myself for entertaining such thoughts.

What the hell am I thinking? Didn't I tell myself over and over that I would never do such a thing again?

No one else would ever allow me to do anything remotely like that. I can't repeat that failed love.

I'm done—I'll never become codependent on someone who doesn't even care for me again.

But...

"I love you," she says, her face still against my chest. "I love you. I love you, Kazuki. That's why...I never wanted someone like him to do that to me."

"—Oh."

After "Nana Yanagi" disappeared, there was something I turned over and over in my mind, each and every day.

What if she had said she loved me?

If so, things would most likely have turned out completely different.

I knew it was a cowardly fantasy, an attempt to explain away my crime against her.

But even though I understood that, I still wanted to know.

I still wanted to know her hypothetical answer.

"......I love you......"

Yanagi says she loves me.

If I don't betray her here, then I'm sure she'll accept me. And if that would lead to a happy outcome, then would I—

—finally be free of that part of my past?

"...I'm sorry to be so sudden."

She finally looks up at me. Her eyes are red from the tears, but they are no longer empty. They contain a firm resolve.

She steps away from me and sits on the bed. I sit next to her.

On this bed, Koudai Kamiuchi took Yuri and—

Before I can think any further, she puts her right hand on mine. I take her hand and squeeze it.

"...I...don't want that to happen to me again...ever."

"...I know."

Her suffering is so apparent to me it hurts.

"...I— I'm going to say something horrible now. But please...don't hate me for it."

"I could never hate you."

She speaks quietly, as if she's truly worried I'll hate her for what she's about to say.

"Help me."

"—That's something horrible...?"

She whispers, "I want you to make helping me your top priority. Do you get what I mean?"

I'm still confused, so she keeps going, her eyes downcast.

"You're the Revolutionary, aren't you?"

...Oh, so that's what she means. *"Are you telling me to kill Koudai Kamiuchi?"*

Yuri goes quiet as I put it outright.

"But killing him is—"

"I know!"

Yuri cuts me off with a yell. I'm startled by this uncharacteristically loud outburst from her, and she lowers her eyes awkwardly.

"I know… If there's any other way, I want to try it. Killing him seems like an awful solution. But is there any way around it? Is there any other way to prevent that from happening to me again—to allow us all to survive? Or are you saying you still think there's some way to persuade him?"

"That's…"

I can't say it. Even I know there's no getting through to him at this point.

But is that really enough to warrant a subjective decision to end his life?

…There's no way. No matter how hard I may find it to forgive him, how many reasons I can list to justify killing him, how much everyone says it's the right thing to do, my life would change the instant I killed him.

And then, my normal life would be gone, never to return.

So I can't do it.

I can't do it, but—

"Don't betray me."

I…

I thought I was waiting for this chance for so long. I thought I was waiting all this time for the chance to fix the past.

The truth is that I already knew.

I knew the reason Nana Yanagi behaved that way wasn't just because she wanted me to comfort her after her troubles with Toji.

She was truly hopeless as a person, but even she was at least aware that there was something twisted about the love she had for Toji. She wanted to do things over and have a proper relationship with someone else, I believe.

Unable to do anything about her feelings for Toji on her own, she had me lick up her tears. She stole my heart exactly according to her plans.

I think her methods were wrong.

But that doesn't mean her feelings were false.

I knew what she wanted to do. I knew, and I pretended I didn't.

After all, Toji was my best friend, and Yanagi was his girlfriend. That's why I couldn't even acknowledge I had feelings for her.

It was impossible for me to do what Yanagi hoped I would.

That doesn't change the fact that I knew how she felt, though. It doesn't change that I knew this yet still decided to ignore it. It doesn't change that I abandoned her.

And so, in the end, the sin rests with me.

Yanagi closes her eyes, puffy from crying, and turns her lips toward me.
Nana Yanagi used to make a face like this.
I can't pretend like I don't notice any longer.
I have to respond to Yanagi's feelings.
I take her shoulders in my hands. Her delicate frame jumps slightly. I close my eyes, bring my lips close to hers, and—

—No.

I open my eyes, not moving any closer.
The word was so sudden, and I'm not sure where it came from. I don't know why I thought this way, either.
Still, that curt voice sounded exactly like hers.
Maria.
……That's irresponsible of you, Maria. If it were you, what would you do?
I can curse her all I want in my mind, but that won't change the outcome. I can no longer do what Yanagi wishes.
Yanagi is still waiting for our lips to touch. After some confusion, I kiss her on the cheek. She opens her eyes, seemingly satisfied with just that.
The kiss on her cheek tasted of tears.
Still, I wonder why?
Despite the taste, they do nothing to quench the thirst in my throat.

▶Day 6 <C> Kazuki Hoshino's Room

The situation progresses, though I still have yet to decide on a course of action.

IROHA SHINDO HAS BEEN EXECUTED FOR FAILURE TO OBEY THE TIMETABLE.

•Iroha Shindo, compulsorily executed for failure to return to her room by 5:40. Died via decapitation.

▶Day 6 <D> The Common Area

There are two hemp sacks on the table in the common area. Their contents are the same as mine, except for the color of the wristwatches, which are black and orange. They're the ones Daiya and Iroha wore.

Koudai Kamiuchi snatches up the four days' worth of rations, two from each sack, as if it was the most natural thing to do.

Despite what I'm seeing, it still hasn't sunk in with me that Iroha is dead. What happened? Noitan lets us know when time is up, so how could she have made a mistake like that?

"It's gotta be suicide," says Koudai Kamiuchi. "She couldn't take the heat, so she stayed put and got executed on purpose is my guess. Probably felt she'd rather be dead than let me get my hands on her. Man, Maricchi and now her. So many rude people here."

Iroha committed suicide?

Something about it doesn't sit right with me. We only spent a few days together, but I just can't imagine her choosing that option.

As for Yuri, it apparently has yet to sink in, as she dazedly picks up the orange watch and stares at it. Maria is watching her with a questioning glimmer in her eyes.

"Yanagi." Maria calls her name

Yuri still seems stupefied when she turns to Maria, who continues:

"Aren't you sad?"

At that, a hint of emotion creeps into Yuri's expression for the first time. Her eyes grow moist, and she crouches down on the spot, covering her face.

"......"

Maria shakes her head and looks away, as if she can't stand the sight of her.

"That's so nice of you to let her know when it's her cue to cry."

"...Hmph." Maria makes no attempt to hide her loathing, snorting angrily at Koudai Kamiuchi.

"Cold as ice... By the way, Hoshino." Koudai Kamiuchi shifts his gaze toward me. "You're the Revolutionary, right? If you want to, you can kill me during the next time block. Which is why I'm gonna have to ask you to die during this one, but..."

Thud.

He stabs a knife into the table.

"You wanna try to stop me? Go ahead. Well, I do have a knife, and you're empty-handed. Hey, actually, I'm game if you all want to try to take me on at once."

"...Three on one?"

"Go for it, if you think you can beat me that way."

...It's no good. For all Maria's skill in the martial arts, she still isn't that gifted physically. Maybe if we had time to come up with a plan it would be worth it, but as we stand now, I can't imagine a violent confrontation with an armed Koudai Kamiuchi would end well for us.

"In other words, big shot, you're as good as dead."

Koudai Kamiuchi pulls out the knife stuck in the table. He then turns the point toward me and grins.

"—Well, thought I'd try saying it anyway."

I'm not sure what he's getting at, and confusion overtakes me.

My face must look funny, because Koudai Kamiuchi starts cackling.

"I was thinking, and I realized that crushing you like this is just boring, you know? So how about we spice things up a bit, eh?"

I have no clue what he's talking about. I don't care at all about winning or losing or boredom or whatever.

"Let's make a bet."

He carries on without a care for the scowl on my face.

"As you know, during the upcoming <E> time block, you can use your Assassinate command, right? The way I figure, you aren't going to Assassinate me, regardless. So that's what I'm betting on."

"......?"

"Look, if you Assassinate me, naturally, I'm gonna die, okay? And then, obviously, I lose, see? On the other hand, if that time passes, and you don't use Assassinate, then we'll call that a win for me. That's all I'm getting at here."

"...That doesn't make any sense. What the hell type of bet is that? There's nothing in it for you. Do you want me to Assassinate you?"

"Not at all. I thought I just laid it out for you. Crushing victories like this are a drag."

"That's what I'm saying doesn't make sense."

"Oh... Well, lemme see. Do you understand how it can feel good to take a risk just for the sake of it?"

All I can do is frown.

"I know it'll never happen, but let's say I compete in the World Cup, okay? I shoot on the goal and score a point. My team wins. Even though I might be a real scumbag normally, this is enough for me to become a huge star and have all that completely ignored. On the flip side, if I screw up and allow the other team to score on us and Japan loses, I'll be so despised I might as well be an actual criminal."

That's definitely a high-risk, high-return competition. Almost exactly like gambling.

"You're the type who avoids games like that, aren't you? Because you're afraid of having everyone hate you. Well, I'm the complete opposite. My adrenaline would be flowing. I'd love to give it a go."

...Yes, I think I'm beginning to see it now. But—

"...Betting your life is...crazy," I say.

"Well, it may be a bit over the top, yeah."

"First off, what are you hoping to gain by wagering your life?"

"Don't we have some prizes right here?"

"Huh?"

No one explained anything at all about prizes to me.

"I knew those prizes from the moment I saw them. I get the feeling I even mentioned it, too."

I remember the very first thing he said. I also recall seeing it several times on my device. I'm pretty sure it was—

"Yo... Hey, do I spy three pretty girls? Lucky me!"

"...You can't be serious."

"I've already had a taste of one. ☆"

None of us would ever hope for *Kingdom Royale* to begin. That's what I had thought. I firmly believed that was the right approach.

That was a mistake, though. Koudai Kamiuchi has been having a blast with this from the get-go.

"I can't figure you out. There's no consistency to your behavior. What exactly are you trying to do here?"

"That's what they're always saying to me."

Koudai Kamiuchi answers Maria's question with an enormous grin.

"They say 'What do you want to do?' or 'Set some goals for yourself' or 'Take things more seriously,' but they should all just mind their own business. Who gives a crap about that? I've got more skills than all the people trying to lecture me anyway. I wish those incompetent schlubs would spare me their inferiority complex BS."

"I see. So you're a true-blue idiot," Maria cuts in.

"Watch your mouth."

She becomes quiet at the sudden cold change in his tone.

"Okay, let's get back to our little bet, Hoshino. So we're both putting lives on the line, got it? As for the prizes, I decided to level the playing field a bit even though I already had this game in the bag, so you don't mind if I'm the only one who gets them, right?"

As if he would let me refuse.

"All you gotta worry about is putting on a good show."

I know he didn't have anything good planned. But even then—

"You just need to let me watch Yuri kill you."

—what he says goes leagues beyond what I had imagined.

"......What do you mean?"

"Exactly what I said. I win the bet, and naturally, we all get to head into tomorrow's <C> block unharmed. I get to have more Private Meetings, aka playtime, with my dear Yuri here. Then, she and I will work together to Murder you."

"What're you talking about? Don't you know Yuri is the Prince?"

"She's the King," Koudai Kamiuchi says plainly.

"Huh? But that's—"

I stop short. Yuri looks up at me, her face a sickly white.

"...Yuri...?"

"I-it's not what you think... Kazuki, it's not!"

Why? Why is she trying to explain herself before I've even said anything?

"Here, let me lay it out for you. Yuri lied about her Class. She and the president switched classes for the big reveal."

"...Why?"

"To survive, why else?"

Yuri's white face is all I need to know he's telling the truth.

"If she's so scared of dying that she's willing to pull a stunt like that, then I know she'll cave to my threats. It'll be easy to get her to use Murder."

"……I won't do it."

Yuri's voice is a whisper.

"You won't use Murder? Heh-heh, sure you will, sweetheart."

"…D-don't mock me. I don't want that to happen to Kazuki, and I can't do it. How can you be so confident that I will…?"

"Because you're the type of girl who offers up her body in exchange for her life, aren't you, Yuri?"

She stops speaking and tenses up.

"There isn't a doubt in my mind that you'll kill to stay alive."

"That's not—"

"Hey, how about I tell the others what you said when you were begging for your life?"

Yuri's eyes widen.

"Any pure-hearted boy who heard the things coming out of your mouth wouldn't touch you with a ten-foot pole."

"……Stop."

"You're really something. Not an ounce of pride in you. I gotta admit, I'm an underclassman with fantasies about girls, and even I was shocked."

"St… Stop, stop, stop……!! Don't say any more!!"

Yuri starts sobbing immediately.

"You cry at the drop of a hat… Don't worry. I was just kidding."

That doesn't stop her tears, of course. Koudai Kamiuchi spreads his hands in disbelief.

"Anyway, whether you trust her is your choice, but I wouldn't if I were you."

I glance over at Yuri as she continues to cry.

I feel bad for her, but if she might Murder me, I can't help but wonder. She did devise a scheme to lie about her Class, after all. I'm sure she won't be able to resist if he dangles the death threat in front of her.

That's how badly Yuri doesn't want to die.

"That's all for the bet. Participation is mandatory. It's not like you have anything to lose, right?"

Having smugly brought the discussion to a close, he puts his arm around my shoulders in a friendly gesture and pulls me toward him, like he's about to kill me.

What the…?

The moment I think this, he shoves something into the pocket of my pants. When I look at him, he presses his pointer finger to his lips. Since he has his arm around my shoulder, Yuri and Maria didn't see.

Completing his objective, he steps away from me.

I stick my hand into my pocket. I feel something crinkly.

Paper…? Maybe it has a message he didn't want the other two to know about…?

"Kazuki."

I quickly pull my hand out of my pocket. Maria continues without paying any particular attention to the action.

"I'm sure it's okay, but I'll just say it anyway." She looks me square in the eye, then says, "Don't kill anyone."

…I knew it. That's what I thought she'd say.

No matter the circumstances, no matter who we're dealing with, Maria will never hope for a resolution due to someone's death.

"……I don't want to, but what am I supposed to do? I'm not worried about myself. But if I die, then you and Yuri will be…"

"And you want to sacrifice yourself for us? Surely you understand. If you use Assassinate, let alone kill someone, you'll never escape the clutches of the Game of Indolence for the rest of your life."

I should understand this.

The moment I kill Koudai Kamiuchi, I'll never be able to return to any semblance of normality.

Still—

"Please don't betray me."

Yuri is still sobbing.

As I watch her in this state, the words I said so long ago play through my mind like a refrain.

"I can't see you anymore."

I'll never do anything like that again.

I will never make a mistake like that ever again. That's why I have to do something, or else Yuri—

"You don't need to worry about saving us, Kazuki."

It's like her words pierce straight through my heart, and I lower my eyes.

"You don't need to sacrifice yourself for that. All you need to worry about is protecting your own life."

"…But if I lose the bet, then I'll be killed."

"Don't worry."

Maria says it as if it's the most natural thing in the world.

"I will protect you."

▶Day 6 <E> Kazuki Hoshino's Room

Before I even read the note, I already knew whatever was on it wouldn't be good.

Kill Yuri, and you're home free!

I didn't expect it to be this horrible, though.

Yuri *is* a Class opposed to mine, the Revolutionary. The same goes for Koudai Kamiuchi as the Knight. On the other hand, the Revolutionary and the Knight can coexist. As far as the game goes, there's no reason for me to kill Koudai Kamiuchi.

So what's he up to?

Maybe he figures giving me this note will get me to Assassinate Yuri, and that's why he made this bet with me?

I wish he would quit belittling me.

I crumple the note into a ball and toss it on the table. I then turn my attention to the monitor.

PLEASE CHOOSE A TARGET TO ASSASSINATE.

I recall how on the first day, I never would have been able to make such a choice.

But now—

I don't know. I have no idea what I should do.

But the one thing I can be sure of is that if I don't do something, I won't be able to save anyone.

...So should I actually kill Koudai Kamiuchi?

That would equate to giving in to the Box. To losing. And then—to never being able to have a normal life ever again.

But maybe that's how it should be? If I can save Yanagi, then maybe the normal life I'm so obsessed with doesn't matter.

That's right. That would make it as if my transgression never happened. If I can redo my relationship with Yanagi, then I—

I...am fine with abandoning normality.

I extend my hand toward the monitor. *Sorry, Koudai Kamiuchi, but I win the bet. I'm going to save Yanagi.* That's what I want. That's justice in my mind.

It's okay, right, Maria? This outcome is okay, right?

I ask the Maria within me, hoping she'll provide me with the answer I want to hear.

Unfortunately, what she says is—

"I will protect you."

—the same thing she said just a little while ago.

"......Oh."

The contradiction stops my hand as it reaches for the screen.

It's true; why would Maria say something like that...? Could I be overlooking something...?

Ah, I get it. Now that I think about it, what was the real reason behind Iroha's death?

It doesn't seem right that she would give up on survival so easily. That's why calling it suicide didn't sit well with me.

What if she was already on the verge of death when she was executed, though? Or what if it was already almost guaranteed she would die?

I pull out my portable device and check the rules.

If someone is targeted for Death by Sword, it'll take effect at 5:55. Iroha died at 5:40. If she knew at that point she was going to get Death by Sword anyway, then...

...wouldn't she try to send some sort of message to us?

...No, that doesn't make sense. Iroha was the King after all. There's no way she would target herself for Murder—

No. I have it wrong. Iroha was the Prince.

The King, the King who is capable of choosing who to Murder, was—

—Yuri Yanagi.

No, no, that can't be it. Let's not jump to conclusions here. The idea that was some message sent from Iroha because she was certain to die is nothing more than an idea I just came up with now.

Still...

I check something on my device.

No doubt about it. Just before that time—Iroha was having a Private Meeting with Yuri.

Iroha broke the schedule and was executed, because she didn't return to her room by forty minutes after the hour. *Because she didn't return from Yuri's room.*

In other words—

—Yuri witnessed Iroha die right before her very eyes.

"Aren't you sad?"

That's what Maria said to Yuri as she was gazing at the orange watch. Then Yuri had started crying as if a dam had burst.

As if she had remembered what she had to do.

"No matter what, I didn't want to die. That's why, so I..."

Because she didn't want to die?

Because she didn't want to die.

"I love you. I love you, Kazuki."

"......"

I reach out for the tabletop and pick up the note I had balled up and tossed away.

Kill Yuri and you're home free!

...Let's say I kill Koudai Kamiuchi here. I'm the Revolutionary, Maria is the Double, and Yuri is the Prince, so of course the game isn't going to end yet.

So then what would she do? Yuri absolutely doesn't want to die, so what would she do if things went down that path?

Koudai Kamiuchi said it earlier.

"There isn't a doubt in my mind that you'll kill to stay alive."

I try to control the almost painful racing of my heart.

"Don't kill anyone."

Why didn't Maria say "Koudai Kamiuchi"?

I scroll through the device again, fearful of what I'll find. I play back Maria's words from before.

"I will protect you."

The recording doesn't change, no matter how many times I play it. Maria knew. She wants to save everyone, no matter who they are, and that's why she didn't say this in front of Yuri while she was crying.

"I will protect you all."

I already know why she didn't say it.

And that's how I—

▶Day 7 <B> The Common Area

"I win."

I lost the bet with Koudai Kamiuchi.

▶Day 7 <C> Private Meeting with Koudai Kamiuchi – Kazuki Hoshino's Room

~~Iroha Shindo~~	Dead		
Yuri Yanagi	→	Kazuki Hoshino	3:40 PM – 4:40 PM
~~Daiya Oomine~~	Dead		
Kazuki Hoshino	→	Yuri Yanagi	3:40 PM – 4:40 PM
Koudai Kamiuchi	→	Kazuki Hoshino	3:00 PM – 3:30 PM
Maria Otonashi	→	Kazuki Hoshino	4:50 PM – 5:20 PM

I never imagined he would choose to have a Private Meeting with me.

"I could tell from your face. You realized the truth and decided not to Assassinate me."

Even though his life had been at stake, Koudai Kamiuchi addresses me as jovially as ever.

"...You were confident I would?"

He grins. "No way! I told you, didn't I? Taking risks gets me off."

I don't think I'll ever be able to understand the way his mind works.

"So maybe you're thinking we should take out Yuri? ...Or maybe not. If you were, you would've done it yesterday, I guess. Heh-heh, she really freaked when I told everyone she was thinking of killing you yesterday, didn't she? ...She was so cute."

"...Why?"

"Huh?"

"Why did you say it like that? You could've told me what she was up to in a way that was easier to understand."

Koudai Kamiuchi's tone is light.

"You know I can't do that."

"So why?!"

"Because I'm head over heels for her." It sounds like another one of his dumb jokes. But his eyes tell me he isn't lying.

"...You realized she's using you? You also realized she's trying to kill you, right?"

"Yeah."

"And you still say you're in love?"

"That's what I said, isn't it?"

He's crazy. No sane mind would think that way.

"What's with that face? She tried to do the same thing to you, didn't she? You know how I feel, then."

"There's no way I—"

"Okay, then did you consider killing her, even just a little bit?"

"...That's..."

My mouth closes of its own accord... No. That wasn't because it was Yuri. I would never be able to kill anyone.

...All the same, it's true that I was a mere step away from killing Koudai Kamiuchi. And yet, I didn't have even the slightest intention of doing the same to Yuri. Even after what's come to light here, I still don't have any desire to.

"Sweet little Yuri has charmed us both despite her attempts to deceive us. We're in the same boat, aren't we? I totally get wanting to stay alive, so I can let her trickery slide... Well, guess that means I'm gonna keep getting played, even if I am onto her schemes. Phew... Gotta hand it to her, Yuri is the biggest powerhouse in this game."

We're still being played.

...He's right. I suspect Koudai Kamiuchi is just cooking up another yarn to try to fool me. Or at least, that's what I hope.

So I ask another question out of a desire to crush this naive notion.

"...How long have you and Yuri been working together?"

"Since our Private Meeting on the first day. It was her idea for me to act so dangerous."

So it really was from the very beginning. Yuri had been searching for a way to survive since the start, when she was white as a sheet.

"...And was it Yuri who instructed you to kill Daiya?"

"Yep. The truth is, she really bought into the whole idea of Boxes and said that this would end if we knocked out Oomine. She seriously believed it."

"Boxes...?"

Even though she kept saying she couldn't believe... Ah, I see now. That was another part of her act to protect her from suspicion.

"You remember how I was looking at my device right before that? What I was actually doing was reading back over my orders from her."

"Just how much did Yuri tell you to do?"

"She told me what to generally say and do. All so that no one would suspect her. Not that she explained that to me, though."

Yuri had been happy and smiling up until Kamiuchi caused that incident.

Even though she knew what would happen next.

"...Maria."

"Huh?"

"Why didn't Maria say anything even though she knew you two were working together?"

"Oh, you picked up on that, too?"

Maria had a Private Meeting with Koudai Kamiuchi right before that. It's possible he did something to keep her from speaking up.

"Fact is, Maricchi got wise to us yesterday. Well, she wasn't certain, more just suspicious. So during our Private Meeting, she started prying into how Yuri and I were connected."

I suddenly remember a comment Maria made:

"You've already had Private Meetings with Yanagi four times, correct?"

"...No way..."

Was Maria already suspicious of Yuri at that point? Did she have doubts about her actions even then, about how she was halfway forcing me to have Private Meetings with her?

And regardless, I neglected Maria's warning and had a Private Meeting with Yuri because I was still haunted by my past with Yanagi.

Which means I invited this worst-case scenario upon us.

"Don't you think Maricchi is a bit too straightforward for her own good, though? You'd think she'd be aware that talking to me about Yuri would put her in danger."

I'm sure she does, but Maria doesn't have any other method of attack.

"Well, it didn't seem like we could keep our secret anymore, and it was getting to be a pain anyway, so I decided to come clean. Oh, and as you guessed, I made her keep quiet."

"...How? Maria isn't the easiest person to intimidate. She's not the type to go along with threats, even if her life is at risk."

"Very true. Maricchi said she wouldn't play along no matter what happened to her... Which is why I took you hostage."

"......Huh?"

"Hey, it's not like I planned to, okay? All I did was reveal to her the honest truth that I was going to kill you next. Then she proposed the idea herself. She said, 'I'll go along with what you say and keep the truth hidden as long as you let Kazuki live. In return, you can kill me.' She's as brave as they come."

Ah, I get it now.

"I will protect you."

She meant exactly what she said.

"I told her, 'Gotcha.' But I don't have any intention of keeping my word. I mean, what's the point? It's not like Yuri is gonna let a Class opposed to hers like the Revolutionary live anyway."

...I'm sure Maria's more than aware of that. She has to know that taking my place doesn't solve anything.

Even then, she can't forsake me.

That's the strength of her pride.

But—

"She's actually a bit stupid, Maricchi."

—Koudai Kamiuchi could never comprehend this.

He's about as far removed from that dignified strength as a person can get.

"...Kamiuchi."

"What?"

"Would you not have killed Daiya if Yuri didn't order you to?"

He answers right away.

"No way."

It probably wasn't a very difficult question for him.

"All she did was give me a little push. I probably would've done something similar even if she didn't give me the knife. I mean, come on, are we supposed to just let time run out?"

He sounds like he's having fun.

"Can't let all this entertainment go to waste."

Yeah, I understand now.

Yuri's behind-the-scenes manipulation and all that doesn't really matter. All I know is that I can never forgive this person. Never.

Watching me out of the corner of his eye now that I've gone quiet and clenched my fists, Koudai Kamiuchi begins digging around in his hemp sack.

"I feel kinda bad for you here, so I'll give you this."

He's holding out a knife.

"...What're you trying to pull?'

"Just a means of self-defense, so take it. As it happens, Yuri says she doesn't intend to pick someone to Murder until your Private Meeting with her begins. If you take her out ASAP, you might get out of this alive, huh?"

"...Are you serious?"

"...Huh? Are you weirded out that I'm helping you? I just feel for you, man. Consider it a parting gift from me, as a fellow member of the Victims of Yuri Yanagi Society."

"That's not what I'm talking about! I mean...you said you love Yuri, right?"

He looks at me blankly, as if he hasn't the slightest idea what I'm getting at.

Oh, I see now.

For him, he has nothing worth protecting. I can't see anything that would form the core of his heart. That's why his behavior seems inconsistent. He thinks nothing of just letting me know how he shut Maria up, or that Yuri is conspiring with him in secret.

I'm done. I don't feel like talking to him anymore.

"...I don't want it."

"Okay."

He tosses the knife on the table without the slightest hint of emotion.

And that's how our conversation ends. Koudai Kamiuchi sits down on my bed, pulls out his portable device, and begins fiddling with it as if he's bored. I crouch on the floor as I would in gym class and press my face into my knees.

I don't want to talk to him, but I still need to confirm a few things.

"Kamiuchi," I ask without lifting my head, "are you going to kill Yuri after I die?"

Yuri and Koudai Kamiuchi are the King and Knight respectively, so it's impossible for them both to survive. If he wants to win the game, he'll have to kill her.

Koudai Kamiuchi answers, "Honestly, I don't know."

He says it so easily, in the same nonchalant tone of voice.

"Might as well leave that as part of the gamble, too, eh?"

I lift my head and look at his face.

He's wearing his ever-present flippant expression. Not a thing about Koudai Kamiuchi has changed. He doesn't feel an iota of guilt for murdering Daiya and Iroha.

"...Hey, this is the first time I've ever said this to anyone, but there's something I have to tell you," I say.

"Knock yourself out."

Taking a deep breath, I muster up all my loathing.

"I hope Yuri kills you."

▶Day 7 <C> Private Meeting with Yuri Yanagi – Yuri Yanagi's Room

The Yuri I once knew is already gone. Her lovable expression has vanished from her pallid face, and now she just looks exhausted to the core.

And her eyes have gone empty once again.

They're the same eyes I saw yesterday before she embraced me. At the time, I thought it was because she was hurt.

But I was wrong.

They were vacant because she was suppressing her emotions to continue the act.

Now—I can't possibly associate this girl with Nana Yanagi.

...No, I probably will never be able to combine them into one, no matter what face she wears.

I already knew from the time I kissed her on the cheek.

When I realized her tears didn't taste like Nana Yanagi's, when my thirst wasn't quenched, I knew.

I simply stare at the girl in front of me.

I watch her intently, as if to say I'll never take my eyes off her, yet without any sort of emotion.

This pale girl clutches her chest. Her breathing is ragged and strained.

She has interpreted my unreadable gaze the way she wants to. That's when I sense it.

She's aware of her sins.

Seemingly dizzy, she wavers, staggers, then presses her hands to her mouth. The effort is in vain, though, as vomit spews from between the gaps in her hands.

"Ungh, gurgh..."

All I do is stand and watch her puke, not even trying to help.

I want to hate her.

I want to hate her.

I want to hate her, the one who deceived me for so long and drove me to desperation. That would be the easiest way. Another way would be to recognize her as an enemy. I need to hate her.

Despite this, by vomiting in utter disgrace, she pleads with me.

"It hurts."

She pleads.

"It hurts, it hurts, it hurts, it hurts, it hurts it hurts it hurts it hurts it hurts it hurts it hurts it hurts it hurts hurts hurts hurts hurts hurts hurts hurts hurts hurts."

"......"

So what? Yuri's the one who drove others to suffer. It serves her right if she's in pain because of her actions. Maybe this show of misery here is just another part of her plan. Only an idiot would feel misguided sympathy for her here.

Even so—

"...Are you alright?"

—I find myself addressing her gently and rubbing her on the back.

"...I'm sorry."

Now that I think about it, she's always apologizing.

"I'm sorry."

After she offers the apology I'm so used to, she continues, *"I'm still going to kill you, though."*

I know that.

I know she won't give up her life so easily after she's hurt herself so much to keep it.

"...Yuri, maybe you should lie down?"

I offer because she seems so miserable, and she complies meekly and goes to lie on the bed. But she still won't let me see her face.

Then she asks me a question.

"...You aren't going to fight back?"

"No."

I'm surprised at how clearly I say it. I reply immediately, even though I hadn't decided whether I would let her go until we met.

But I'm fine with that. I'm positive the word that left my mouth so quickly is my answer.

"...Then why did you decide to have a Private Meeting with me?"

"Because there's one thing I need to ask."

I tell her why I chose to meet with her and not Maria.

"Please don't kill Maria."

I can hear Yuri's breath catch in her throat.

"...Why do you think I would kill Otonashi? I'm the King, and she's the Double. She's a Class I don't need to kill to survive the game."

"You tried to get Koudai Kamiuchi to kill me, right?"

"......Yes."

"If I killed him then, the game still wouldn't have ended. In fact, you wouldn't have been able to ask him to get rid of me. Whichever of us was killed, in the end, you would've had to act directly. In that case, why would you go to the trouble of trying to convince me to kill him?"

I hurl the accusation at Yuri as she lies there, quiet and motionless.

"It's because you think it'd be easy to kill someone like me, right?"

Her head jerks a bit.

"If you're going to kill one of us with a knife, then it's too great a risk to leave him alive. There's pretty much no danger with me. That's why you wanted me to live. Am I wrong?"

Yuri remains silent for a time, she but responds in the end.

"......You're not wrong."

I'm actually a bit shocked that she admits it so readily. But I keep that feeling hidden.

"Now, though, you're stuck. You have no choice but to try to kill someone you don't stand a chance against in a direct confrontation on your own, and with a knife, no less. What're you going to do? How are you planning to increase your probability of survival?"

"......"

"...I already know what you're going to say. To better your chances—*you're going to use Maria Otonashi.*"

Yuri curls herself into a ball on the bed.

"I don't know exactly how. As much as you've done, though, there's no reason to expect you'll go easy on her at this point. At the very worst, I'm sure you'll even murder her if that's what it takes to survive."

I bring my face close to hers and look her in the eyes.

"That's why I'm begging you."

For the second time, I make my request.

"Don't kill Maria."

I won't let her look away. I must get her to promise me this, at least.

Her eyes empty, she answers in a slightly tremulous tone.

"...Promises are easy to make. I can just lie or something, so all I have to do is promise."

"......Huh?"

"You'll already be dead by the time I start planning how to use Otonashi, so you won't be able to tell if I'm keeping my promise. So there's no point saying that to me now, is there? Surely you already know by now that I lie when I have to."

She could've just made the promise and let things end here, but for some reason, she's going out of her way to warn me.

"...You're not like Koudai Kamiuchi."

"Huh?"

"You actually have some concept of guilt. That's why I know you'll cave under the threat I'm about to make."

Threat. Her eyes go wide at hearing that violent word from my lips.

"If you kill Maria—*I will destroy your life.*"

It's true I won't be there when Yuri breaks her promise. But that doesn't mean I won't be able to threaten her.

All I need to do is set a trap that will spring if she fails to keep her word.

"If you kill Maria, I'll curse you and see to it that you continue to suffer. I'll become a ghost haunting you, showering you with curses twenty-four hours a day, never allowing you to forget for even a moment that you are a murderer. I'll make your life worthless and obliterate you completely."

At the force in my voice, Yuri's face crumples into an expression somewhere between laughing and crying.

"She's important to you," she whispers. "She's that important to you."

Yes, this was good. She understood the purpose of what I was doing.

"Yeah... That's why I'll never let you live it down if you kill her."

It's a threat that works precisely because Yuri has a sense of wrongdoing.

She knows that the instant she murders Maria, she herself will die of guilt.

Yuri won't kill Maria now.

I step away from the bed and sit on the table. "...So why'd you decide to have a Private Meeting with me?"

"......"

"You chose me for a Private Meeting, too, didn't you?"

Yuri looks at me where I sit.

"Yes... I did." Her gaze moves to the ceiling. "There's one last thing I want to speak with you about. I'm sure this might be difficult, but will you listen to all the horrible things I've done? ...Well, but you've found out about most of it on your own."

"...Are you trying to repent?"

"No. I would be much more comfortable keeping all of this hidden."

"Then why do this?"

"Because it'll help you."

I frown. "It'll help me? What will?"

"Learning how I created this situation, the details—it'll help."

I don't see the point. I'm gonna die soon, after all. It doesn't matter whether anything helps me or not.

Regardless, Yuri begins to speak, not answering my last question.

"I was thinking of what I can do to survive from the moment I arrived in *Kingdom Royale*."

Her voice is shaking. Guess she was telling the truth when she said she'd rather not get into this.

"I came up with ways to increase my chances, fearing for my life the whole time. Essentially, at that point I was thinking of how to win the killing game. The conclusion I reached was that I needed to make allies among the people here.

"In particular, I wanted to get the Revolutionary and the Sorcerer on my side. I wanted to find out who had those two Classes. That's why I planned to suggest we all reveal our Class. But unexpectedly, Oomine came along and proposed the idea for me."

"And you wanted to make allies of the Revolutionary and the Sorcerer to..."

"To kill the others."

She says it flat out… I get the feeling she's almost boasting of her own faults.

"But the Sorcerer turned out to be Oomine, and he wouldn't work with me. I'm sure he probably saw through my performance, saying I could turn my tears on and off like a faucet. And then you were the Revolutionary. You aren't the type of person who could easily kill someone even if I asked."

"So that's why you allied with Kamiuchi, the Knight…? You really decided on him quickly, though. He said you were telling him what to do from pretty much the first day."

"I could tell right away that he, um…wanted me. I'm…very alert to that kind of thing. So I got him on my side and then had him do what he did to make the situation feel more dangerous."

"Why did you need to do that?"

"To make everyone feel like something needed to be done quickly. When people think they're in crisis, they start wanting to make plans. I built a foundation for everyone to want to reveal their Class."

I see it now… If everyone felt like the game of murder could never take place, there would be no need for any further actions.

"I surmised that what Otonashi told us about Boxes was true. That's why I had to kill Oomine."

"And so you had Koudai Kamiuchi do it, even though it took an extra bit of effort."

"Yes. However, *Kingdom Royale* didn't end even after Oomine died. For that reason, I shifted my goals from killing the owner to winning the game. You know pretty much all the rest, right?"

I nod. I'm almost certain I do… But I still have one question.

"What about Iroha…? Was her death a dying message?"

I can see that Yuri's face is openly tense.

Her look tells me Iroha's death had some special meaning to Yuri. Though she spoke so smoothly of her own deeds, it seems this topic is difficult for her to discuss.

Yuri bites her lip once, but she eventually speaks.

"…I think it probably went as you imagine. We had targeted Iroha for Murder. When she learned this, she let herself die that way so that you and Otonashi would know about my scheming."

Her voice is faint—evidence of a conscious effort to fight down her emotions.

I'm suddenly aware of something. The watch on her right wrist. Her original watch was beige. But—the one she has on now is orange.

"Even in a game like this...I can't beat...Iroha..."

Silence overtakes her.

I get the feeling Yuri won't answer any other questions I may ask about Iroha. That's why I decide to stop pursuing that topic.

"I get how you manipulated behind the scenes... But I still don't understand. How is what you told me just now supposed to help me?"

The question prompts Yuri to get up from the bed and regard me with those empty eyes.

"...Why do you think I believed in Boxes?"

"Huh?"

"Can I ask you to trust me about what I'm going to say next? ...No, I'm sorry. It's wrong of me to ask that of you after how much I've betrayed you." She continues hesitantly, "But you asked, so I'm going to tell you. *I have memories of what happened right before I came to this place, which none of the rest of you have.*"

"—!!"

My eyes go wide at this unexpected revelation.

"I received an explanation from the owner telling me we would be playing a game of murder called *Kingdom Royale.*"

The owner...? Is she saying she knew the identity of the mastermind who made us play this *Kingdom Royale* all along?

"...And this owner is...?"

She tells me.

"Oomine."

Daiya is the owner...?

I swallow... No, this isn't far from what I imagined. Rather, with a little thought, it makes sense. The reason she believed Maria's explanation was that she knew Daiya was the owner. But—

"But—the Box hasn't been destroyed, even though Daiya is dead."

That's right. If Daiya is the owner, then the Game of Indolence should be finished.

"I thought it would end there, too. I think that's how it was explained to me. However, as you know, it didn't. That allowed me to figure out the answer right away."

She explains.

"The Oomine who was here is not—'Daiya Oomine.'"

"...What're you saying? Who is that Daiya, then?"

"That's..."

Suddenly, she stops short.

"...I'm sorry. I'm not going to say. If I do now, I'm afraid you won't believe me. Just think about it. I won't call it proof, but the Oomine here didn't seem to be aware he was the owner of this Box, right?"

"That's probably..."

If Daiya did know, he'd never let himself be killed in such a pitiful manner.

However, undeniable as that fact, it still doesn't make everything Yuri has been telling me the truth. I can't determine how much of what she is saying is fact.

"Yuri, I'm gonna die soon, aren't I?"

"Yes."

"Then when will I be able to believe the parts of your story that I can't believe now?"

It's an unanswerable question, so maybe it's a little mean.

But she replies straightaway.

"When your turn comes."

"My turn...? What do you mean 'my turn'...?"

She doesn't respond. I'm sure that this, too, falls under her category of things I "can't believe."

Could it be—that even if I die, even if Yuri wins, *Kingdom Royale* doesn't end? Does it reset and start again? Just how long will it continue?

Don't tell me it's...until the owner is satisfied...?

"Are we gonna end up fighting each other again like this...?"

Yuri averts her eyes after I say this.

In place of an answer, she says, "...Kazuki, I have a single favor to ask of you, okay?"

She looks as if she could break down into tears any moment.

"Okay, I'll listen."

"Thank you. Then make me a promise. Whether it's the next time, the time after that, or even the final time, your turn will come without fail. When it does, I'm sure you and I will face each other again. And when we do—"

She stands up. Swaying and tottering, she walks up to where I'm sitting on the table.

"When— When we do—"

Tears stream from her eyes.

"—please kill me."

She clings to me. It isn't so much a hug as it is just throwing herself limply over me.

"You must, *must* kill me. If you don't, I'll never be able to forgive myself. No... I'm probably past that point already, but I'll hate myself even more. So you have to kill me. To let me meet you again. Please. Please, please, please—"

"—don't betray me."

That's when it dawns on me.

Just maybe, I might be able to redo this all over again. Maybe there is a chance for me to survive.

But despite that—I can't save Yanagi.

Watching her as she cries, I recall Nana Yanagi again. I had seen her and Yuri Yanagi as one and the same. If I fell in love with Yuri and saved her, then I might be able to change those events of the past. That's what I had believed.

That was never possible, though.

They're two completely different people, and even if I saved one, it wouldn't mean I saved the other. The only reason I failed to notice this obvious fact, one that anyone could have figured out immediately, is that I didn't want to.

I wanted to be saved myself.

But I understand: This Box was born to stave off someone's boredom, and there's nothing here that will save me.

"Sorry, but I will betray you."

I say it plain and clear.

After all, I'm sure—I will forget Yanagi once again.

"Even when my turn arrives, I won't kill you."

Yuri's suffering may continue even after *Kingdom Royale* ends.

But I've made my decision. I'm going to protect what matters, and this Box won't beat me. Neither will my past with Nana Yanagi.

Me as I am now...

...Maria...

...and my normal life—I will protect them all.

...Huh, seems like things always work out that way for me.

"I see...," she whispers with her face still downcast, and she returns to the bed. She then turns her back to me, hiding her face from view.

I address my question to her back. "...Can I ask you one thing, too?"

"What is it?"

"Are you confident you can beat Koudai Kamiuchi?"

After this, she'll have to face her final opponent, Koudai Kamiuchi. She has to kill him, and she should have no chance of winning against him in a fair knife fight.

"......Of course I am," she says, turning around.

"......Oh."

I'm shocked.

Her eyes aren't empty anymore. The charming smile has returned to her face.

Naturally, this is not an authentic expression. That's why I'm so stunned.

I mean, she can hide all that suffering so cleverly, completely fooling us all.

"It might be different if it were Iroha or Otonashi, but you don't seriously expect me to lose to a half-wit like him, do you?"

Unlike Nana Yanagi, this girl used me without growing dependent on me, and she's grinning as she gives me her caustic answer.

"I will fool him, and then I will kill him."

"...I see."

I can't help but smile, even though she had made a fool of me so many times. And then I remember:

"I'm scared... So scared."

"No matter what, I didn't want to die. That's why, so I..."

"Help me."

She certainly deceived me. However, she had lied to me as much as you might expect. Her fear, suffering, and desire to be saved were all genuine.

And—

"Kazuki."

—Yuri Yanagi is smiling as much as she did when I kissed her on the cheek.

"I...loved you, Kazuki."

▶Day 7 <C> Private Meeting with Maria Otonashi – Kazuki Hoshino's Room

I tell Maria everything I know.

No matter how hard this outcome may be for her to accept, she can't do anything about it.

Yuri has already chosen me as the target for Murder. Maria knows this can't be changed.

For that reason, we simply sit on my bed, our hands clasped together. As if trying to remember the shape of each other's hands, we squeeze them over and over, intertwine our fingers, and just savor the sensation.

For the last time, we feel each other's touch.

"Kazuki."

Maria says my name.

"The truth is, I've been keeping something from you."

"...Huh?"

"I don't have the Misbegotten Happiness now."

Not sure why that's significant, I simply look at her.

"I can't be certain, but I feel it may have simply lost its power temporarily. I've encountered something like this before; however, it's possible this could be a characteristic of the Game of Indolence."

...Wouldn't that be considered, y'know, pretty huge?

"Why didn't you tell me?"

Maria looks down for a moment, then explains with our fingers interlinked.

"I am a Box, not a human. I've explained to you often that I exist for others. Maria Otonashi... No, Aya Otonashi must exist this way. What supports me in this is the Misbegotten Happiness. Despite this, I can't call upon it here. So what am I?"

"You're...Maria."

"...So this is how it is now?" Maria squeezes my hand so hard it hurts. "I can't even protect you anymore?"

"...Maria."

"Hmph, some Double I am. If only I could die in your place."

Maria's bad habit is rearing its ugly head again.

It's that horrible tendency to put herself down so quickly.

"...Stop. I would never want that."

"I know! I know that desire is purely my own selfishness!" she shouts.

My eyes go wide at how blunt she is about it.

"...What?"

So she's aware of it herself? Didn't she honestly believe that all she did was to the benefit of others?

"You let me know that several times during that week not so long ago. This is simply my own pride at work..."

With that said, Maria fixes me with a stern gaze.

"But still! I'm still a Box!"

I can't help but fall silent in the face of her intensity.

She knows, but she still can't change herself. The reason is the firm resolve within her. If that were to change, then I have no doubt she would no longer be able to remain who she is.

"......Sorry for yelling." Maria looks away awkwardly. "It's just that it frustrates me. I can't accept this outcome."

"...It's okay, Maria. If what Yuri says is true, we will meet again."

"I don't care. That doesn't do anything to change the fact that the Kazuki here in front of me will be gone. Right now, I'll lose you, and that's certain."

"......Maria."

I find the idea of coming back to life hard to believe, too.

"...Kazuki, as I just told you, I can't say that I'm a Box as I am now. Which is why I can't protect anyone. It's possible all I'll be able to do from here on out is watch Yanagi suffer. Within *Kingdom Royale*, I'm just a powerless girl," Maria says. She reaches up and cradles my head against her chest. "That's why, even if it's just a little, I think it's okay for me to express Maria Otonashi's true feelings."

She whispers to me.

"I'm sad."

Her lips brush against my ear.

"I can't stand the thought of you dying. It pains me. I hate it. It hurts. I want to be with you."

I suddenly remember when I knelt and extended my hand to her within that classroom of endless repetitions.

"I may be powerless. I may be nothing more than an ordinary Maria Otonashi now. But—"

Back then, though only for the briefest moment, she had been a mere powerless girl.

And now, within the Game of Indolence, she is helpless again.

"—But I still want to protect you, even if it means throwing away my life."

I can't see the expression on her face as she says this.

But I do know the answer I need to give.

"I'm sorry."

I made this decision when I chose Maria instead of Yanagi, after all.

"No matter how much it hurts, it's not your job to protect me here."

I decided when I chose her, the one who made me who I am now.

"When you don't have your box, it's my job to protect you."

I will defend Maria.

And I will defend my normal life.

I will defend the normal life that Maria doesn't want.

▶Day 7 <C> Kazuki Hoshino's Room

And then, I am run through by an invisible sword.

•Kazuki Hoshino, dead via Death by Sword

************** GAME OVER **************

- Winners

Yuri Yanagi (Player)
The King; killed Kazuki Hoshino on the seventh day by choosing him for Murder, killed Koudai Kamiuchi directly on the same day. Survived.
*Victory conditions were fulfilled by the deaths of Iroha Shindo, Kazuki Hoshino, and Koudai Kamiuchi.

Maria Otonashi
The Double; survived.
*Victory conditions were fulfilled by the death of Kazuki Hoshino.

- Losers

Iroha Shindo
The Prince; executed for failure to follow the schedule.

Daiya Oomine
The Sorcerer; died due to hemorrhagic shock after his carotid artery was slit with a knife by Koudai Kamiuchi.

Kazuki Hoshino
The Revolutionary; died via Yuri Yanagi and Koudai Kamiuchi's Death by Sword on the seventh day.

Koudai Kamiuchi
The Knight; killed Daiya Oomine directly on the sixth day. Killed Kazuki Hoshino with Death by Sword on the seventh day. Died due to hemorrhagic shock after being stabbed in the abdomen with a knife by Yuri Yanagi on the same day.

Kazuki Hoshino

Maria Otonashi

Iroha Shindo

Yuri Yanagi

Koudai Kamiuchi

Daiya Oomine

START GAME

▶Day 1 <B> The Common Area

I heard this was a game of kill or be killed.

I thought I was appropriately attuned to the danger.

But there's no way I can deal with this. No one could imagine this sudden game over.

The knife pressed against my throat digs in. I'm on the floor, and I can feel blood flowing down the back of my neck.

"I got distracted."

A girl with nice features is speaking in front of me.

"I got distracted when I saw it was you, Kazuki. I suppose it's because some part of me wanted to help you. Maybe that means I'm still immature."

This girl is simply blinking like some sort of machine without the slightest change in expression, and what she's saying means absolutely nothing to me.

She loosens the grip on her knife a bit, then continues:

"Anyway, I'm gonna tell you about myself for future reference. Only until that bastard Kamiuchi arrives, though, so it won't be much. Damn, guess that means he's alive, huh? He's the one I really wanna kill."

What is she talking about...? Who is Kamiuchi? Hell, who is she? Why does she know my name?

"I don't have any amazing physical abilities, and my IQ isn't off the charts. My memory isn't photographic, and I don't experience synesthesia. I don't have a single one of those easy-to-understand special abilities. So why am I the way I am?"

The blood-drenched girl tells me with no emotion on her face.

"Because I have focus."

She carries on matter-of-factly.

"Take the sprint, for instance. The first thing I do before I run is clear my mind of distractions. I block out everything, like thinking I can beat so-and-so, or that I'm at a disadvantage, or that winning here could take me into the national tournament or whatever. I simply analyze what an ideal run for the day will look like by examining things like the condition of the track and the state of my white muscles, along with the rest of my body, and then I run a mental simulation. Once I'm crouched in the starting position, I focus exclusively on sound. I ignore all extraneous noises, and I concentrate solely on the crack of the pistol. Sound travels around 1,125 feet per second, though, which is slow. I actually start as soon as I hear the very beginning of the shot, but I can't do that in my head. So I base my start on the feeling of overtaking the sound itself. I run according to the simulation I put together beforehand. No excess thought is needed. That's why, after I run in a tournament, I have no memories of the sprint itself."

Having said all that, she turns her emotionless eyes toward me.

"Oh, sorry. I guess I got a bit long-winded. The main point is that by channeling all my energy in a single direction, I can summon abilities that people might call exceptional. I'm good at that, end of story, so I'm not a superhuman. Yeah, I suppose that information will prove helpful to you."

I can't make any sense of it. She must have lost her mind.

I realize the back of my head is wet. I can deduce what type of liquid it is, but I can't check to be certain… And I don't want to.

Something else catches my attention.

"Uh, ah—!"

Maria's body is lying on the ground.

And she's not the only one. I see other prone, motionless forms, too.

"I might be angry, just a little. Koudai Kamiuchi's atrocities are one thing, but then there's that stupid bitch, too. She tricked me without a care in the world, not just in this game, but in regular life, too."

I'm not sensing any anger or other emotions from her expression, though.

"That bitch Yuri said she hung around with me because she knew I liked her. And she didn't even like me. She just wanted to make me suffer. She's horrible. When she told me about it, I couldn't come up with any plan besides a dying message even though I knew they were gonna kill me."

I'm through trying to make sense of what she's talking about.

"Still, I don't think those emotions had any influence over what I did here. You don't need emotions to win this. I was already prepared by the time they finished explaining *Kingdom Royale*."

"......Prepared?"

"Yeah—*prepared to maintain the focus needed to keep killing until victory is certain*."

Then, without the slightest change in expression...

...she kills me.

I begin to lose consciousness soon after she slits my carotid artery.

As I slip away, maybe it's just my mind playing tricks on me, but I think I hear a wailing scream. As the voice enters my ears, I finally remember.

Right, she's the student council president.

•Kazuki Hoshino, dead via slit carotid artery inflicted by Iroha Shindo

************ GAME OVER ************

• Winners

Iroha Shindo (Player)

The Sorcerer; killed Yuri Yanagi, Maria Otonashi, Daiya Oomine, and Kazuki Hoshino directly on the first day. Survived.

*Victory conditions were fulfilled by skillfully surviving.

Koudai Kamiuchi

The Double; survived.

*Victory conditions were fulfilled by the deaths of Kazuki Hoshino and Maria Otonashi.

• Losers

Yuri Yanagi

The Knight; died due to hemorrhagic shock after her carotid artery was slit with a knife by Iroha Shindo on the first day.

Daiya Oomine

The King; died due to hemorrhagic shock after his carotid artery was slit with a knife by Iroha Shindo on the first day.

Kazuki Hoshino

The Prince; died due to hemorrhagic shock after his carotid artery was slit with a knife by Iroha Shindo on the first day.

Maria Otonashi

The Revolutionary; died due to hemorrhagic shock after her carotid artery was slit with a knife by Iroha Shindo on the first day.

The intoxicated wavering ceases, and the transparent hands controlling me vanish.

In front of me is an arcade game cabinet with *Kingdom Royale* written on it.

I'm back in that black, dark space. The sinister, sticky air that seems to cling to my body fills me with loathing—and then I remember.

That's right. Those transparent hands came out of this machine and grabbed me, and then—

"Welcome back from the meaningless slaughter."

Daiya Oomine, the owner of the Game of Indolence, stands before me.

"So how were the Replays?" Daiya asks.

"Replays...?"

"Yeah, everything you underwent in *Kingdom Royale*, you didn't actually experience. How should I put it...? Okay, it's like you were living through something like the records or backlogs of other players."

What the hell is Daiya talking about? The records of other players? If I was, then why was it all from my viewpoint?

Those memories were undoubtedly mine.

"I can see you don't really understand."

"...I mean, those were definitely my—"

"Those were NPCs."

Daiya answers straightaway.

"...What?"

"Don't you know any gaming terminology? Okay, what I'm saying is that thing you thought was you was actually an enemy controlled by the *Kingdom Royale* computer. If that wasn't the case, you definitely wouldn't be here after dying twice, right?"

...I don't understand. The me who went through all that suffering and mental anguish was just an NPC?

"...You're lying. There's no way it could copy my behavior and thoughts so realistically."

"It can. That's what makes it a Box."

"...You may be right, but..."

Now that I think about it, Maria didn't have her Box. Could that be because she was an NPC?

"...But why would you do all this?"

"I thought I told you? This Box, the Game of Indolence, is made to simply force people into the game of *Kingdom Royale* and fight off boredom. *Kingdom Royale* won't start unless there's a human to start the killing. If it doesn't start, it's no good as a diversion. So what do I need to do to guarantee one person kills another?"

Daiya tells me, without allowing me to get a word in.

"I build a system where one person will always kick off the slaughter."

"Why does having NPCs make it so one person will always start killing?"

"In *Kingdom Royale*, only one player is fighting in the true sense. If they lose, then they die. All the rest are NPCs. You still with me?"

I nod, a frown on my face.

"The player knows the other people are NPCs. They're hard to tell apart from the real thing, but the player knows that even if they kill the NPCs, the originals are still alive. *On the other hand, they also know that for them, and them alone, it's all over if they die.* Now then, do you think a player in that position would be able to go without killing anyone?"

I remember something Yuri said during the second game.

"I don't want to die."

She must have been the player in that game. I wonder if she would've done what she did if she had no clue what was happening... My guess is no. I'm positive she was influenced by the knowledge that everyone else was an NPC.

No, what's really worrying is Iroha. She was much more open about it.

She suppressed her emotions and ended the game as quickly as possible because she knew she would have a chance to do it over again. Each of the three games unfolded in a completely different manner. Everything can change so much depending on the player, and that's undeniable proof that the player is the key to starting *Kingdom Royale.*

"...So why did Yuri suffer so much and try so hard not to kill us? She would've known we were NPCs, right?"

"You really are a slug with no imagination. You do know those NPCs are perfect copies of you all? True, you can kill them, and the real versions won't die... But on the flip side, that's the only difference."

"...?"

"The NPC of you isn't different from the real you in any way. Its personality is exactly like yours in every way possible. Would you be able to forgive someone who killed a being identical to you? Or to look at it the other way, would you be able to casually murder someone else's NPC?"

I close my mouth.

"You know the answer because you did the Replays. Killing an NPC feels the same as killing the real thing."

...He's right. Whether the real me was alive didn't matter a whit to my NPCs. Yuri and Iroha killed those other "me"s.

The NPCs and I are identical yet separate beings.

"...Daiya, is it fair to say that the experiences of the NPCs based on me in these Replays you're talking about can be treated like my own experiences?"

"Yeah, I don't see any issue with that."

If so, that means I have yet to win or lose *Kingdom Royale.*

What will decide that is yet to come.

I look at the arcade cabinet before me.

Next time, I will play *Kingdom Royale* in the truest sense. I'll play a game where there are no do-overs, where dying means dying.

"It's your turn."

"So the players up until now have been Daiya, Yuri, and Iroha in that order, right?"

"Yeah, what about it?"

"What are Yuri and Iroha doing now?"

"They're in the darkness here. Sleeping, or maybe I should say 'stopped.' If you looked around, you could probably find them, but you won't be able to do anything, so there's no reason to. You'll only go free once all the six player games are over."

"And they're all alive?"

"Yeah. Because they won as players."

"...The memories of our time playing *Kingdom Royale* aren't going to vanish, are they?"

"No."

I remember. I didn't actually experience those things, so maybe that isn't the right way to put it, but...at any rate, I remember.

Yuri Yanagi's empty eyes.

Iroha Shindo's wail.

They'll suffer, bear the guilt of their actions, and never be able to rid themselves of it. I won't be able to save them, no matter what I do in my upcoming game.

I cannot help them anymore.

Just like them, the only one I can help is myself.

...No, that's wrong.

"Daiya."

"What?"

"When is Maria's turn?"

Daiya replies.

"After yours."

I see. Then—

—I can save Maria.

I look around, searching for her form. I know she should be in this space. But I'm completely surrounded by that unpleasant gloom, and I can't see anything except the immediate vicinity of the arcade cabinet.

Yuri and Iroha gave me hints in the hope that I would win. They taught me strategies on how to defeat them.

But that won't work for me.

After all, Maria has no chance of winning. She can't carry out the killing and deception essential to this game.

Within the Game of Indolence, she is powerless.

I have to save her. If I don't, she will become my new Nana Yanagi.

But what do I need to do? Even if I'm victorious in *Kingdom Royale*, that only ensures that I survive and doesn't do anything to help her.

That's right—my goal isn't to win *Kingdom Royale*.

It's to crush this stupid Box, the Game of Indolence.

"...What's that cheeky look for, Kazu?" Daiya scowls at the way I'm watching him.

"......This really isn't fair, is it, Daiya?"

"What?"

"I'm saying it's cowardly."

Daiya seems openly displeased by my comment... Just as I planned.

"How so? I was the very first player of *Kingdom Royale*. I had to feel my way through without any Replays, so when you take that into account, I had the biggest disadvantage of us all. And you call that cowardly?"

"Our objectives are different."

"What?"

"In my case, winning *Kingdom Royale* doesn't mean I've completed my objective. It just means I survived. You know that my true goal is to make it back to my normal life, right?"

"......"

"Killing someone during the game is enough to prevent me from ever reaching my objective. If *Kingdom Royale* doesn't end until you kill somebody, then I'll never be able to meet that goal. There's no winning for me, in other words. Meanwhile, you get to throw me in a cage and watch me invariably lose. Doesn't that sound cowardly to you?"

After I put that out there, Daiya gives me a silent glare. I meet his eyes and hold my stare, fighting to keep my terrified heart in line.

This goes on for a while—but then Daiya bursts into laughter.

"Wh-what's so funny?"

"What're you saying? That little staring contest there was meant to make me laugh, right? Okay, fine, fine, I lose. Your face really does crack me up, though."

"...I'm asking what's so funny about it!"

"It's just funny. You're obviously trying to challenge me to turn the situation to your advantage."

"......Oh."

He sees through my little provocation.

"Try again when you're as smooth as Yanagi. You could never fool me with your crappy acting. You're about as silly and empty-headed as they come."

"Ugh—"

Guess it's no good—

As long as Daiya doesn't change the conditions, I have no chance of accomplishing what I want to do. Had I reached a deadlock?

Will I—not be able to save Maria?

"But it sounds interesting," Daiya says.

"......Huh?"

"What I'm saying is that *I accept your challenge.*"

I still can't process it, though, and my jaw drops.

"There's a secret trick that will allow you to end *Kingdom Royale* without killing anyone."

Daiya carries on without paying attention to me. I manage to close my mouth, then focus on what he's saying.

"Do you remember how that green bear says it'll be boring if everyone gets mummified?"

I sift through my memories.

"AnYWaY_I_wish_you_all_GOOd_luck. DoN'T_let_the_game_end_with_some_bORIng_outCOme_where_YoU_are_all_muMMIfied."

Yeah, he did say that.

"I'm repeating myself here, but this Box is meant to fight off boredom. It doesn't want a peaceful end where nothing happens. It doesn't take into account the idea that the game could end without any murder because that's not interesting. And so, the moment it's certain no one will be killed, the game shuts down. Everyone's food runs out, and when the time comes, the player will be released."

"So in other words—"

"If no one kills anyone else for eight days, you can survive."

Yeah, there it is.

That will be the proof I've beaten the Box and taken back my normal life.

"And—if you reach that ending, I'll destroy the Game of Indolence. This is your idea of fair, right?"

"...Really?"

"When have I ever lied?"

...Plenty of times, actually.

But I'm pretty sure he'll keep this promise. As prideful as Daiya is, there's no way he'll break a promise in a contest with such clearly defined rules of victory or defeat.

Victory is no longer an impossibility for me.

Of course, keeping everyone, including Daiya and Koudai Kamiuchi, from killing others is going to be an extremely difficult task. Someone might make a mistake as time runs out, and the fear of death runs high. The road to the ending that's only available after eight uneventful days is going to be rough.

Even so, I have no other choice.

"...Daiya."

I jab my pointer finger at him.

Daiya has been calling *Kingdom Royale* a "meaningless slaughter."

However, I reject that idea.

It does have meaning. The struggles of Yuri, Iroha, and all the others taught me how to defeat Daiya.

I won't let their pain be for nothing.

"I will beat you, Daiya."

Daiya laughs boldly and declares:

"Not a chance in hell."

AFTERWORD

Hello, Eiji Mikage here.

This is the third *HakoMari!* book (I tried giving it a cute abbreviation). The guy who has always seemed a bit suspicious is finally starting to take the stage. He's an easy character to write, so I've been waiting for him to take an active role more than anyone.

Now then, here's something that simultaneously touches on the plot but doesn't.

I've managed to get three books out in this series so far, but the truth is I went through quite a few rejections before it got off the ground.

There was even a completely finished story that was entirely rejected.

That rejected story will never see the light of day. I thought it was interesting, but it died before it ever got to reach any readers.

But that's as it should be.

I was of course shocked and frustrated to have the story I spent months writing get turned down, but I think it lives on as the nutrients that helped my current works grow... Maybe that sounds a bit dramatic, but it's undeniable that I wouldn't be where I am now without several failed works under my belt.

If I had given up on writing, those failed stories would have truly died where they were.

When I think of this, it makes me realize how important it is to keep going without giving up. But I think I'm getting a bit too serious here. Oh yeah, for those of you who have yet to read the story, this time it's about six boys and girls who live together for a little while and do a lot of shouting as they play a game. Sounds fun, huh?

Now for my acknowledgments.

To Tetsuo, the illustrator, thank you once again for the awesome drawing despite your busy schedule.

To my editor Kawamoto, thank you for everything up until now. I've grown a lot thanks to you. If you'd like, I can write a BL for your department! ...Sorry, that's lie. I can't do it.

And to all my readers: With this book ending the way it does, I hope to have the next one out before you know it. It'll be out in the spring! Or...I think it will be. It should be. It'll be nice if it is!

See you next time!

Eiji Mikage